A Candlelight Ecstasy Romance®

**"IT'S ALL OFF, JOE. I WOULDN'T MARRY *YOU*
NOW NO MATTER WHAT YOU SAID."**

"What's wrong, Lynne? Tell me what it is and give me
a chance to explain."

"You've already explained everything just beautifully.
You don't want a wife. All you want is a ranch hand. You
want someone to clean your fish and deliver your calves
and nurse you when you're sick. Well, you can count me
out, Joe. I want to be *loved!*"

"But I do love you, Lynne. You've got to believe that."

"I *don't* believe it. You didn't even love me enough to
buy me an engagement ring." She wiped her eyes, streaking mascara across her cheek. "I once thought you really
cared for me, but I should have known you couldn't ever
love a woman as plain as I am—maybe no man could.
Well, I learned my lesson. I'll never make the same mistake again."

CANDLELIGHT ECSTASY ROMANCES®

MORE THAN SKIN DEEP

Emily Elliott

A CANDLELIGHT ECSTASY ROMANCE®

Published by
Dell Publishing Co., Inc.
1 Dag Hammarskjold Plaza
New York, New York 10017

Dell ® TM 681510, Dell Publishing Co., Inc.

Candlelight Ecstasy Romance®, 1,203,540, is a registered
trademark of Dell Publishing Co., Inc., New York, New York.

ISBN: 0-440-15821-4

Printed in the United States of America

First printing—February 1986

To Our Readers:

We have been delighted with your enthusiastic response to Candlelight Ecstasy Romances®, and we thank you for the interest you have shown in this exciting series.

In the upcoming months we will continue to present the distinctive sensuous love stories you have come to expect only from Ecstasy. We look forward to bringing you many more books from your favorite authors and also the very finest work from new authors of contemporary romantic fiction.

As always, we are striving to present the unique, absorbing love stories that you enjoy most—books that are more than ordinary romance. Your suggestions and comments are always welcome. Please write to us at the address below.

Sincerely,

The Editors
Candlelight Romances
1 Dag Hammarskjold Plaza
New York, New York 10017

CHAPTER ONE

Lynne Kosler yawned as she whipped her brand-new Fiero into the parking lot of the Brownsville Immigration and Naturalization Headquarters. As usual, she was just barely on time for work and she didn't want her boss, the chief patrol inspector, to have reason to call her down for being late. As one of only two women border patrol agents in the Brownsville office, she was very much aware of the extra attention being paid to her work by her superiors, and she wanted to make the best impression possible. Easing her six-foot frame from the sports car, she reached back in with a long arm and retrieved her dark-green hat, which she positioned on her head before walking into the building's large conference room where the agents met with their chief before starting their duties of the day.

Lynne needn't have worried. Most of the other agents were milling around, drinking coffee and talking with the agents who had just gotten off the night patrol. She poured herself a cup of coffee and sought out Bert Garza. "How was it last night, Bert?" she asked, smiling.

Bert shook his head. "We tracked a bunch of them through pasture for six hours, but we lost them about Raymondville."

"Sorry about that," Lynne said, looking down at the short, muscular agent. "How's Patsy doing?" Bert's wife Patsy was due to deliver any day now.

"Tired and grouchy and big," Bert griped. "I don't know who will be happier to see this baby come—her or me!"

"I'll talk to you in six weeks, when it's kept you up crying half the night," Lynne said, winking at Bert.

"And how do you know so much?" Bert teased.

"I have a ten-year-old brother and I remember well," Lynne said. What she didn't add was that she and her older sister Laura had raised Dennis for the first six months of his life while their mother had recovered from a blood clot in the lung.

"Well, our baby's going to be different," Bert vowed. "A real little angel." He winked back at her and they both laughed.

"Mornin', Lynne, Bert," Drew Evans drawled as he ambled up to them. At six foot four, Drew was one of the few men in the office taller than Lynne. He grinned at them both with his lopsided smile and Lynne smiled shyly back. "How was it last night, Bert?"

"We lost them," Bert admitted. "I wish one of you had been with me." Both Lynne and Drew were known for their tracking skill, while Bert was better at undercover work.

"Who knows, maybe one of us will be next time," Drew said, sipping his coffee. Suddenly his eyes widened; he had spotted another green-clad figure coming through the door. "I swear, here comes a sight for sore eyes. Mornin', Suzy, come over here and let's have us a little talk."

Lynne watched impassively as Suzy Bender strode

10

across the room, her stunning figure apparent even in her no-nonsense uniform. As she stepped up to Drew, he reached out and engulfed her in a huge bear hug. Drew lowered his voice and exaggerated his drawl. "Woman, you want to have an affair?"

Suzy looked up at him with a considering expression and pretended to think a minute. "Tell me," she said slowly. "Do you wear Jockeys?"

Drew stepped back and appeared to think. "Why, yes, ma'am, I do."

"Then forget it," Suzy said. "I have had it up to *here*" —she stopped and held her hand up level with her eyes— "with people who wear Jockeys!"

Drew, Lynne, and Bert started to laugh. "What's the matter, Suzy, are Ron and the boys giving you a hard time at home again?" Bert asked. Suzy often laughingly complained about being the only woman in an all-male household.

"This morning it was a pear down the toilet," Suzy explained. She rolled her large blue eyes. "And Ron wants to get a dirt bike! Can you believe it?"

Drew laughed and put his arm around Suzy again. "Well, honey, you know where you can come anytime it gets to be too much for you," he said. "Now, are you sure about that affair?"

Suzy made a production of checking her watch. "Sorry, Drew, I just don't have time this morning," she said with mock regret. "Maybe tomorrow." She unwound Drew's arm and walked over to the coffeepot.

Drew rolled his eyes in mock regret. "Well, a man can dream, can't he?" He sighed watching Suzy's shapely figure stride across the room.

I guess a woman can dream, too, Lynne thought rue-

11

fully as she looked at Drew's long frame. Bert left for home just as Ben Miller, the chief patrol inspector, walked in. Never one to insist on a lot of formality, he poured himself a cup of coffee while the agents gradually sat down. Lynne found a chair near the door and watched Jack Perkens, another of Suzy's admirers, pour her a coffee and set down beside her, flirting outrageously. As Ben took his place at the podium, Lynne thought wistfully that it must be nice to have men falling all over you all the time.

Lynne sipped her black coffee and watched Drew sit down across the room. If she had been like Suzy, he would have come over and sat by her. Ben cleared his throat and began to speak, but for once Lynne was listening with only half her attention as Ben gave instructions and made assignments for the day. She looked first at Drew Evans, who she'd had a mild crush on since coming to work here three years ago, and then at Suzy Bender, as Suzy made careful note of Ben's instructions. Suzy was a real knockout, Lynne had to admit as Suzy's full lips curved into a smile at Ben's risqué comment. And Lynne had to admit to herself that she was just a little envious of Suzy.

It certainly wasn't that Suzy said or did anything out of line. Far from it. Suzy was a hardworking agent and a model wife and mother, and fended off the more obvious flirting by making reference to her husband and children. But Drew and half the agents in the office were smitten with Suzy's good looks and showered the woman with masculine attention. As she stretched her long legs in front of her and folded one over the other, Lynne wondered what it would feel like to attract men that way.

Lynne smiled to herself, picturing the face she saw in

12

the mirror every morning and night. She could wonder every day for the rest of her life what masculine attention felt like but she would never know, for the face that stared back at her was never going to stop traffic. Her face was plain, there were no two ways about it. Her mouth was thin and rather stern, even with the application of lipstick. Her only redeeming feature was her large, expressive hazel eyes, but most of the time their expression was guarded, their beauty hidden.

It wasn't that she didn't try to look nice. She got up every morning and carefully made her face, and although she had to wear her light-brown hair in a long braid while she was in uniform, she had it professionally styled once a month. But even with the effort she made, there just wasn't much she could do to make herself into the raving beauty Suzy was, or that most of the men in the world apparently wanted. They were not interested in looking past Lynne's plain face to see who was inside.

Lynne listened as Ben droned on, and watched Suzy shifting her shapely body in the chair. If only she had a good figure, she might attract a little interest. But Lynne stood an even six feet, and no matter how much she ate, her figure remained thin and angular. In an effort to fill out a little, she had even taken up weightlifting last year, which had made her stronger and better at her job but had created no new curves.

Oh, well, I guess some of us have it and some of us don't, Lynne thought as her eyes roamed the room. And she had to admit that her fellow agents had been perfectly nice to her, subjecting her to none of the male chauvinism she had expected when she and Suzy had started work as the first two women agents in the office. But they treated her as one of the boys, the same way men had treated her all her life. That must be the way they saw her. She guessed that by the age of twenty-six she ought to be used to the lack of attention, but it still hurt a little sometimes.

Turning her thoughts from her own shortcomings, Lynne heard her name mentioned and immediately gave Ben her full attention. She was to partner Drew today on a highway stakeout. She glanced over at Drew and he nodded toward her, just as he would have nodded toward any partner. She figured she had another day of listening to him talk about his pretty girlfriends, and wondered what Drew would think if he knew that she would like to date him herself. Ben wrapped up the meeting, and the agents began to file out the door to their particular assignments for the day.

Lynne and Drew were just leaving the room when Ben's secretary rushed through the door with a piece of paper flapping in her hand. Ben quickly scanned it. "Lynne, Drew, come here for a minute," he said, motioning them over. "I have something here I want you two to check out before you set up your stakeout."

"Sure—what is it, Ben?" Lynne asked.

"We just got a telephone call that there are some illegal aliens working out at the Stockton ranch. Better go out and check."

"I wonder if the new owner knows enough to check for an alien registration ID," Lynne said. She took the paper and looked at it.

"Prob'ly not," Drew drawled. "If what I heard's true, he's a city boy and only been out there a couple of months."

"Well, go check it out and then get out on the high-

14

way," Ben said. "This time of year they're coming over in droves."

"What makes April special?" Lynne quipped. "They come over in droves all year long." She and Drew left Ben and walked out to the parking lot where the border patrol cars and paddy wagons were parked. Most of the cars were gone, but there were three paddy wagons parked in a row. "We'd better take a paddy wagon," Drew said.

Lynne nodded. "There's probably somebody out there who needs a ride back across the border."

"Poor devils," Drew said as they were climbing into the front of the paddy wagon. "It must be pretty dismal over there for so many of 'em to try to come over here."

"You know it is," Lynne said softly. Contrary to what the illegal aliens probably thought, Lynne and Drew and most of the other agents felt genuinely sorry for the people whom they were paid to apprehend and send home. For unlike most other branches of law enforcement, where the agents dealt with true criminals, in most cases Lynne and her fellow agents dealt with people who only wanted a better life for themselves and their family. Although border patrol agents certainly met up with their share of criminals and violence, most of their charges were docile and often not upset by their capture. The aliens knew they would be sent back to Mexico, and from there they would have another chance to try to sneak into the United States. Lynne could sympathize with their desire for a better life, while at the same time she felt that it would be much wiser for them to try to come over legally.

Drew swung the paddy wagon around and out of the parking lot. "So what have you heard about the new owner of the Stockton ranch?" He pulled a package of gum out of his pocket and withdrew a piece.

"Oh, a few things," Lynne answered, taking the stick of gum that Drew held out to her. "He's from Dallas, I heard."

"Yeah, I heard the same," Drew said. "I also heard that the rest of the family was fit to be tied when old man Stockton up and left the whole ranch, lock, stock, and barrel, to this one nephew. They were looking forward to splitting up the profits from a sale."

"And he doesn't intend to sell?" Lynne asked.

Drew squinted his eyes against the early-morning sunlight. "Would you?" he asked. "I can only dream of a break like that." On several occasions in the past when Drew and Lynne had been on long stakeouts together, Drew had spoken of his desire to own a ranch someday.

"No, I wouldn't," Lynne said softly, thinking of the ranch on which she had been brought up. "But what might seem like a treasure to you or me might just be a pain in the neck to a city boy. So he hasn't sold it yet?"

"No, and according to Hannah Michaels he doesn't intend to. He moved in last month and she says he plans to make it his livelihood."

"And what else did this Hannah say about 'him'?" Lynne teased, knowing that Drew loved to gossip almost as much as he loved to flirt with Suzy.

Drew grinned. "Well, for starters, 'him' is named Joe Stockton; he's about my age, single, and according to Hannah, a man who looks like him is bound to be a playboy. Anyway, Hannah says he's had several good-looking women down to see him since he moved."

"Yes, I remember something about the good-looking

16

part," Lynne mused. "The girls at the health club were drooling about him one evening."

Drew sighed and cracked his gum. "You know, you women are all alike. You don't care a thing about what's on the inside, you just want a fancy package." Drew ran his hand through his thick red curls and down his broken nose that had never quite straightened after its encounter with the fist of an illegal alien.

"You think men are any different?" Lynne asked rather acidly.

Drew looked over in surprise at the harsh tone of her voice, but at that moment they reached the turnoff that would lead them into the Stockton ranch. Lynne hopped out of the truck and unlatched the gate. As they bumped down the dirt road that led to the ranch house, Lynne peered around for any sign of life. Except for a mare and her filly grazing in the pasture, the ranch seemed devoid of all life, human and animal alike. At the main house Drew ground the paddy wagon to a halt. "Now comes the fun part," he said. "We get to play the heavies and have everybody mad at us by the time we leave."

"Of course Stockton will be hostile if we deport half his help," Lynne said offhandedly. "They always are."

Together they walked up to the front door of the old ranch house. The house was large and solidly built, with two stories and a big front porch with a swing, but the front step was broken and the dingy house desperately needed a coat of paint. This would be a nice place if the new owner would fix it up a little, she thought as Drew knocked on the front door. Maybe he intended to. After all, he hadn't been here too long.

Drew knocked again, but there was still no response from inside the house. "Well, let's go looking," he said.

17

They walked around to the back and spotted a shiny new Trans Am parked beside an old, dilapidated pickup truck. "That's as bad as that souped-up number you drive," Drew said under his breath. "Look," he said, gesturing toward the pen back behind the barn, where a veritable beehive of activity was taking place. "Looks like the party's over there."

As Lynne and Drew got closer, Lynne could hear the small group of men speaking to one another in true Mexican Spanish rather than the Tex-Mex that most Mexican-Americans used. Five would get you ten they all ended up in the paddy wagon, although none of the men seemed too perturbed when they saw her and Drew approaching in their telltale uniforms. When they reached the lot, Lynne saw a cow on the ground in the center of the group, and a man kneeling in the mud beside her. One of the Mexicans spoke to the kneeling figure in broken English, and the man stood up and walked toward the gate of the lot, leaving the Mexicans staring down at the cow. As he opened the gate and stepped out, his straw hat blew off his head, bouncing a few feet before lodging against a fence post.

That man has the most beautiful head of hair I've ever seen in my life, Lynne thought as he approached her and Drew. Thick and straight, it was just the shade of shining, champagne blond that women spent a fortune for in the beauty salon. Lynne stared for a moment at his gorgeous hair; then she lowered her gaze to his face as he walked toward them. Even covered with dust and dirt his face was one of the most wickedly handsome she had ever seen in her life. This had to be Joe Stockton, she thought as she took in the piercing, bright-blue eyes, the wide, smooth forehead, the small, perfectly straight nose. His

18

full mouth was set in a frown of displeasure at the moment, but Lynne could see that it was well shaped, and for a brief moment she wondered what it would feel like pressed against her own.

Joe Stockton wiped his hand down the side of his pants and extended it to Drew. "I'm Joe Stockton," he said, his lips curving in the barest glimmer of a smile. "What can I do for you folks today?" He shook hands with Drew and turned to Lynne. She placed her hand in his and shook his firmly, the touch of his work-roughened palm sending unexpected chills up her spine. She looked down a couple of inches to meet those piercing blue eyes and saw the blankness there. Suddenly disappointed, she withdrew her hand from his and her own eyes became even more shuttered.

"I'm Drew Evans and this is Lynne Kosler. We're from INS, and we have reason to suspect that some of your employees are in the United States illegally. We need to check their IDs this morning." Drew spoke politely but firmly.

"Suit yourself. I made sure they were legal before I hired them, but if it makes you feel any better, go ahead and check their IDs. Now, if you'll excuse me, I have a problem over here that needs my attention." He turned on his heel and started back toward the lot. Even though he was not tall, the breadth of his shoulders and the way his back tapered to a narrow waist and hips reminded Lynne of a Greek statue. She felt another surge of attraction for Joe, an attraction she couldn't seem to help.

"We may as well just check them out here," Drew said. He and Lynne followed Joe back to the lot. Joe motioned to the men to get out their wallets before he turned his attention to the cow.

One by one the five men stepped up to the fence, showing Lynne and Drew their IDs. Lynne looked over at Drew and raised her eyebrows. It was possible that the information they had received was incorrect, but in their experience that wasn't too likely. There was bound to be someone on the ranch who wasn't legal. As the men returned to the middle of the lot, Lynne watched them through narrowed eyes, looking for a movement, a telltale flick of the eyes, that would reveal dishonesty or concern. Four of the men seemed perfectly calm and at ease, but one of them, a very young man, kept glancing toward the small row of two-room shacks on the other side of the barn. *He has something to hide,* Lynne thought as she opened the gate of the lot and moved inside. Sidestepping a pile of manure, she gasped when she saw the miserable shape Joe's cow was in. She was in the middle of calving, but the head had presented rather than the front legs, and the calf was stuck halfway down the birth canal. The calf was still alive, but from the blue around its nostrils something had to be done, and quickly, to save it.

She looked at Joe Stockton and over at the men standing around helplessly. "Why doesn't one of you do something?"

Joe turned irritated eyes in her direction. "What in hell do you expect us to do?" he asked. "She's having the calf, not us."

"You mean you don't *know?*" Lynne asked, astonished.

"No, I don't know, and apparently neither do any of them," Joe said, jerking his thumb toward the men, who had moved to one side to make room for Lynne. "They may be legal, but that's all they've got going for them."

"They're probably from one of the cities or the moun-

20

tain towns," Lynne said slowly. "I doubt they know any more about it than you do."

"Great," Joe muttered under his breath.

Without hesitating Lynne took off her watch and handed it to Joe, then squatted down beside the heifer. Not bothering with gloves, she quickly pushed the calf's head back in and groped for the front feet, finding them and pulling them forward. Drew handed her a rope he'd found hanging on the fence, and with a quick motion Lynne tied the little hoofs together and tugged with a steady pressure until the small calf emerged from the heifer's body.

Joe stood there with his mouth hanging open. "Is *that* what you do?" he asked. "I thought they could do it by themselves."

Lynne took a wet towel from one of the workers and wiped off her hands and arms. "Well, most of the time they can, but when their head emerges first, you've got to give them a little help."

Joe handed her back her watch. "I wish I'd known that last week. I lost both a heifer and a calf."

Lynne looked down into Joe Stockton's face and her legs nearly buckled underneath her. He was smiling, really smiling, at her. And he had such a beautiful smile! Oh, there was nothing very sensual in that smile, but his eyes shone warmly and the hint of a dimple dented the slash on the left side of his mouth. She smiled back a little tentatively, her hazel eyes becoming warm. "I'm sorry you didn't know what to do," Lynne said as she brushed the dust off her pants. "I suggest that you let these men go and find somebody who can teach you the ropes."

"You mean some wetbacks?" Joe asked. Lynne's eyes widened before she realized that he was teasing her.

21

Lynne and Drew both laughed. "No, Mr. Stockton, most illegal aliens don't know the first thing about running a ranch," Lynne said. "If I were you, I'd call the employment commission in town and hire a foreman for a few months." Her smile faded and her manner became businesslike. "I thought one of your employees was acting a little strangely earlier, and it's unusual for us to get a report of illegal aliens and find none at all. I need to check out the houses over there."

"Be my guest, but those five men are the only people I have here," Joe said. He knelt down beside the calf, and Drew and Lynne left the lot.

"Since when is delivering calves part of the job description?" Drew teased as he and Lynne walked toward the row of two-room houses where the hands lived.

"It's not, but it was obvious that none of them knew what to do, and I couldn't very well let the calf die, now, could I?" Lynne said shortly.

"And I thought you were just trying to impress old good-looking down there," Drew said.

Lynne's face turned scarlet. "No, not really," she mumbled. "A man who looks like that has his pick of women. He's not going to notice the border patrol agent who comes to take away his help. Besides, he's a good two inches shorter than I am."

"So? Look at Dudley Moore and Susan Anton, Princess Grace and Prince Rainier, Sonny and Cher, Henry and Nancy Kissinger. It didn't stop them!"

Good for them, Lynne thought irritably as they approached the houses. They had left the men with Joe, so the houses should have been deserted, but as they stepped up on the front porch of the first one Lynne thought she heard a noise. She motioned to Drew, who stepped to the back of the second house; she walked quietly to the front. Suddenly, the door opened and a little child no more than eighteen months old toddled out on the front porch. Lynne stood quietly, and just a fraction of a minute later a young woman in her early twenties came scurrying out after him, fussing at him in a gentle torrent of Spanish. Intent on finding her child, she smacked right into Lynne, who reached out and caught the woman by the shoulders so she wouldn't fall.

The girl whitened with terror as she stared up into Lynne's stern face, shaded by her uniform hat. The frightened woman swallowed helplessly, her eyes traveling down the green shirt to where Lynne's badge rested. *"La Migra,"* she whispered as her hand flew to her mouth.

"Sí, soy la Migra," Lynne said slowly in her accented Spanish. *"La Migra"* was the nickname by which illegal aliens referred to border patrol agents, and Lynne knew that she and the other agents were hated and feared by most of them. "Is your husband with you?" she continued, still speaking Spanish.

"No, it's just me and my boys," the woman replied. "Will I have to go to prison?"

Lynne shook her head. "No, just to the deportation center for a night and then back home. Drew! I've got a woman and child here on the front porch."

Lynne could hear Drew coming through the house, and he emerged a moment later carrying a tiny infant. The woman looked at her child in Drew's arms and moaned, looking as if she were about to faint. Lynne swiftly took the baby from Drew and handed it to her. "We won't hurt your baby," she assured the terrified woman. "Do you have any belongings?"

23

The woman nodded, and Lynne followed her back into the house and watched her put one clean pair of panties and an old housedress into a battered suitcase. She put one change of clothing each for the children on top of her own things and shut the suitcase. Lynne looked around, but she could see nothing else that could have belonged to the woman or her children.

Joe and the young man Lynne had noticed earlier were standing outside the shack when Lynne emerged with the girl. The young man was holding the toddler in his arms, and Joe eyed him sternly. "What's going on?" he asked.

He looked at Joe and shrugged. Joe looked from the young man to the young woman. "Sir, I didn't know she was here," he said to Drew. "Honestly I didn't."

"It's all right, you're in no trouble, Mr. Stockton," Drew said. He turned to the young man. *"Es su esposa?"* he asked.

"No, es mi hermana," the young man replied.

Lynne looked from the stricken face of the man to the heartbroken face of the woman, who had tears running down her face. *"No, no quiero regresar!"* she cried, flinging herself into her brother's arms. "I want to stay here!" she cried in Spanish. "I don't want to go back! I just want better for my boys!"

"I'm sorry, but you have to go back," Lynne said in Spanish, pulling the young woman away from her brother as gently as she could. Lynne cringed at the sobs that tore through the woman's body as she put her into the paddy wagon. Drew handed in the infant and the toddler and shut the door.

Joe Stockton stepped up to the paddy wagon. "I'm sorry," he apologized to Lynne. "I didn't know she was here. She couldn't have been here all that long."

Lynne spoke briefly to the young man in Spanish before turning back to Joe. "He says she just got here last night. She was going to try to get to Houston and work as a domestic."

Joe looked from the sobbing woman to the stricken brother. "Is there anything I can do? Sponsor her or something?" He looked at Lynne almost accusingly.

"No, there's really nothing at this point," she said gently. "She'll have to get her papers and come over legally. I'm sorry."

Joe looked up and was surprised to find sincere regret in Lynne's eyes. His own expression softened and he gave Lynne a half-smile. "Thanks again for helping with the calf."

Lynne nodded, and climbed in the truck beside Drew. "No problem," she said. "Good luck with the ranch."

Drew headed the paddy wagon down the dirt road back to town and to the detention center, where the process of deportation would begin. "There are days when this job is the pits," he said, glancing into the rearview mirror at the crying woman.

"Yeah, I feel sorry for her," Lynne said. She looked behind her and watched as Joe Stockton walked back toward the corral that held his new calf.

As they drove back toward town in silence, Lynne's thoughts kept returning to the good-looking rancher they had just left behind. He was unquestionably one of the most handsome men Lynne had ever met, and she felt attracted to him as she had never felt attracted to a man before in her life. In her thoughts she looked at him again, at his shiny blond hair, his bright-blue eyes, his sensual lower lip. Lynne felt desire curl in her lower abdomen as she remembered the way his calloused hand had grasped hers. But when she pictured the expression on his face as he had looked at her, desire faded and vague depression replaced it.

He probably didn't even notice that I'm a woman, Lynne thought dispiritedly, looking out the window at the rolling countryside. Oh, he had certainly been polite enough, and he had been properly grateful to her for getting the calf out of trouble, but he had looked right through her, as all men did. *Darn it, Joe Stockton, why couldn't you have at least winked your eye at me or* something? For the first time in a long time she desperately wished that she had been pretty enough to attract the attention of a man like Joe Stockton.

CHAPTER TWO

Drew pulled up in the parking lot of the detention center. "You know, I hope she makes it back over here," he said, gesturing backward toward the young woman and her children. She had stopped crying, but there were tear-stains running through the dust on her cheeks, and her eyes were blank.

"I hope she does too," Lynne said as she got out of the cab. She unlocked the back of the paddy wagon and spoke quietly and politely to the woman. "I'm sorry we have to send you back, but you must abide by the laws of our country," she said in Spanish to her. "You can try to sneak back in, of course, but sooner or later someone will catch you and send you home."

"La Migra?" she asked.

"Yes, La Migra will catch up with you sooner or later."

"But the man said that it would be so easy! He said we wouldn't be caught, that we would be all right!" she cried.

Lynne's lips tightened. "How much did you pay to come over here?" she asked.

"Three hundred American dollars," she said.

Lynne swore under her breath. Although the amount

was smaller than many people paid, it had probably taken the woman's brother a long time to save it and now it was gone, wasted. Lynne and her fellow agents thoroughly despised the slimy, sneaky people who made fortunes smuggling illegal aliens across the border. Lynne asked the woman a few questions, but she really didn't know anything about the man who had smuggled her and the children across in the back of a pickup truck.

Drew and Lynne walked the woman and her children into the detention center. The woman immediately shrank back at the cold, institutional rooms with bars on the windows, whispering, "Prison," under her breath. Lynne explained that she would be here for a day, two at the most, before she was escorted back across the border. Lynne started to process the little family herself, but Drew reminded her that they were supposed to be on a roadblock, so she handed the woman over to one of the agents on duty.

A little while later she and Drew were parked along Highway 77 between Harlingen and Raymondville, watching for suspicious vehicles or passengers in the lane traveling north. Lynne and Drew patrolled the highway for the rest of the day, stopping a number of cars and taking three carloads of illegal aliens back to the detention center. Most of the aliens they apprehended that day were men coming over to work in the fields, and Lynne didn't feel too sorry for them, but she couldn't quite forget the look of terror on the woman's face. She had wanted to come over so badly, Lynne thought when she and Drew had loaded up their last carload of aliens and were driving back to the detention center. She had wanted a better life for her boys. Lynne's eyes softened at the thought of the plump, bright-eyed toddler who had wandered out of the shack this morning. That little guy deserved better than to be a wetback all his life. She finished her paperwork and picked up a set of immigration forms on her way out the building for the day.

Lynne got into the Fiero and pulled out into traffic. She started to drive out to the Stockton ranch, but changed her mind and turned the corner that would take her to the health club where she worked out. The young man she needed to talk to was probably still working, and she wanted plenty of time with him to explain to him why his sister should wait and come over legally, as he had. Besides, she was tired and frustrated and needed to relax a little before she drove back out to the ranch.

Two hours later, after a strenuous workout, a hamburger for supper, and a much-needed shower and shampoo, Lynne was driving toward the Stockton ranch. Deliberately wearing a feminine blouse with her jeans and leaving her hair free to hang down her back, she bore little resemblance to the stern-faced picture of authority she was in uniform, and she hoped that she could appeal to the man on a less threatening and more human level. Bouncing down the rutted road that led to the ranch houses, she wondered briefly if she would see Joe Stockton again tonight, but shrugged off the possibility as unlikely. He was probably in town by now on a date.

Lynne parked in front of the ranch house and made her way through the dark to the second house behind the barn. Light shone from the windows and Lynne could hear the sound of a Spanish-language station blaring from a tinny speaker. As she stepped up on the porch, she could hear the sound of low-pitched laughter coming from behind the door following a ribald comment about

29

someone's girlfriend. Lynne swallowed back a little apprehension and knocked.

"Entra, Juan," one of the voices called.

"No soy Juan," Lynne called through the door.

Immediately the laughter and teasing comments stopped. One of the older men threw open the door, and five pairs of dark eyes turned in Lynne's direction. Lynne wasn't sure if the surprise and discomfort on their faces was because they remembered her from this morning, or if it was because they hadn't expected to have their card game interrupted by a tall Anglo woman.

"I'm Lynne Kosler," she said in Spanish. "I was here this morning. May I speak to you, please?" She pointed to the young man, who was straddling a chair and drinking a beer.

"La Migra?" he asked, hastily standing up and reached for his wallet.

"No, I don't need to see your ID," she said quickly in Spanish as the other men started to reach for their wallets too. "I brought you some papers. May I talk to you outside for a moment?"

The young man nodded and left his beer on the table. He followed her out to the small porch, where Lynne sat down and motioned for him to join her. "What is your name?" Lynne asked, handing the man the papers.

"Carlos. Carlos Torres. My sister is Consuela."

"Well, Carlos, you know I really didn't want to take your sister away this morning," she said, "but the law of our country says that she must make application and enter this country legally, just as you did."

"But it took me two years!" Carlos protested. "That's too long!"

"I know it takes a long time," Lynne said slowly. "But

it's so much better in the long run if you do wait. Tell me, does Consuela want to stay in this country?"

Carlos nodded. "Yes, we both do."

"Well, Carlos, since you came over legally, you can now do that, if you want to. You can make application in a few years and become a citizen. In the meantime you have many of the benefits of being an American already. You can use our public hospitals, you can use many of our agencies, you can use our public schools. But if Consuela comes over here illegally, she and her children won't have any of that. She can't use the public hospitals if she gets sick, she can't use our agencies, her kids can't go to school. Carlos, those little babies of hers deserve better than being *mojados!*"

"I guess we hadn't thought of that," Carlos admitted. "It's just that Consuela's husband left her last month and she needs to work. She can't find a job in Mexico."

Lynne sighed sympathetically. "I know it will be rough for her while she waits, but I'm sure Mr. Stockton pays you enough to send her a little money to help her along, doesn't he?"

"Oh, yes, I can help her," Carlos assured Lynne. "Can you help me fill out the papers? I can't read too well."

They sat cross-legged on the porch for the next thirty minutes while Lynne asked Carlos the questions on the application and wrote his answers in the blanks. When they had finished, she promised to turn in the application the next day. As she and Carlos stood, the back door of the barn opened and a man walked toward them, his thatch of pale-blond hair shining in the moonlight. Lynne's eyes followed Joe across the yard as he stalked up to the shack, and she swallowed nervously as she smoothed her rumpled blouse. Joe was dressed only in jeans and a pair of tennis shoes, and Lynne gazed with admiration at his broad, firm chest covered with hair as blond as that on his head. Joe peered from her tall figure to Carlos, and his frown of displeasure turned to puzzlement. "What's going on? I thought I heard a woman's voice out here."

Lynne stepped off the porch. "You did," she said. "I came to bring Carlos a set of immigration forms for his sister."

Joe stared up in astonishment at the tall, angular figure standing on the porch. "You're that lady agent who was here this morning?" he asked, extending his hand.

Lynne took his hand and stepped off the porch. "Yes, I'm Lynne Kosler and I was out here this morning. I came to bring Carlos a set of papers for his sister. I was just leaving." She turned to Carlos. "I'll turn these in tomorrow," she told him. "Adios."

"Adios, señorita," the man said shyly.

"I'm sorry if I seemed angry when I walked up," Joe said as Lynne started to walk back toward her car. "It's just that I don't allow them to bring women other than wives on the ranch. Uncle Jack said that saved a lot of fistfights."

Lynne laughed softly. "Uncle Jack had a point."

"I didn't recognize you," Joe said. "You look different out of uniform. Tell me, is this part of your job?"

Lynne shook her head. "No, I just felt sorry for Consuela and her kids," she said. "She only wanted a better life for her children. I talked to Carlos and explained the advantages of her waiting and coming over legally. I hope she makes it."

"I hope she does too," Joe said as they walked past the back door of the ranch house. "Say, would you like a glass of iced tea before you go? I just made up a fresh pitcher."

"Sure, I'd love some," Lynne said, and followed Joe into the brightly lit kitchen of the ranch house. The room was as run down as the outside of the house, but with a coat of paint and a new set of curtains it could be cheerful. Lynne leaned against the counter, crossing one booted foot over the other, and watched as Joe took two ice-cube trays from the freezer and twisted them to loosen the ice. He oozed masculine attractiveness, and Lynne had to stop herself from reaching out and running her fingers through the thick blond hair that covered his chest. Joe filled two glasses with ice and poured the freshly brewed tea over them. "Do you take sugar?" he asked.

"No, but I'd love a little lemon if you have it," Lynne said.

Joe squeezed a little lemon juice and handed her the glass. She followed him through a dreary living room, full of old brown furniture, out to the porch, where Joe sat down on the front step.

"Do you mind sitting out here?" he asked. "That living room's dismal. As soon as I have time, I'm hauling that ugly stuff away and having my furniture from Dallas shipped down."

"Are you really planning to stay? That's what all the gossips are saying."

Joe grinned and nodded. "So I've been the subject of a little gossip, huh?"

"Well, Brownsville's not that big, and the Stockton ranch has been around for a long time," Lynne stammered. "Naturally people are going to be interested."

"That's all right, I don't mind if people talk," Joe said.

"And if you would like to put in your two cents, you can report that you heard it straight from the man himself that I'm staying and hoping to learn enough about ranching to make it my life." Joe's eyes took on a faraway look. "I've dreamed of it for long enough."

"You didn't grow up on a ranch, then?" Lynne asked. She leaned against a pillar and stretched her long legs out in front of her.

Joe shook his head. "No, I grew up in the middle of Dallas. But I did spend my summers here with Uncle Jack and Aunt Ada. He always said he was going to leave the ranch to me because I loved it, but I never believed he'd really do it!"

"I'm glad you got your wish," Lynne said softly.

"And from that little miracle you performed this morning, for which I'm very grateful, I would guess that you grew up on a ranch somewhere," Joe said thoughtfully.

Lynne nodded. "Dad and mother used to own a ranch about halfway between here and Corpus Christi."

"Where are your parents now?"

"My little brother has severe asthma, so they sold the ranch and moved to Phoenix six years ago. My sister and I decided to stay here."

Joe drank a large swallow of iced tea. "Do you miss the ranch?"

"Oh, sure I do," Lynne said. "Although I do like my work, at least most of the time, I miss the ranch life very much. Daddy said that if he and Mother could have made it without the money from the ranch, he would have given it to me." She smiled across at him. "I envy you, you know."

"Sorry about that," Joe said. "Did you learn to ride a horse?"

"Just before I learned to walk, that's all," Lynne said. "I keep Betsy boarded at my sister and brother-in-law's place outside town."

"What kind of horse is Betsy?" Joe asked. "I have two quarter-horses here."

"She's your basic cow pony. Nothing special, but I love her. I guess you ride, too, don't you, if you spent your summers here." Lynne reached up and slapped a mosquito off the side of her face.

Joe nodded. "And I'll have you know I'm better at riding than I am at delivering calves."

"Thank goodness! I wouldn't want you to fall off!" Lynne teased.

Joe blushed in the dim porch light. "All right, all right, I'll learn," Joe said. "I called the employment commission this morning after you left and they put me in touch with a man who used to be foreman on a ranch up close to Laredo. He's coming down to work with the understanding that I can only afford to hire him for a few months, until I've learned enough to take care of this place myself. Think I can learn it in a couple or three months?"

Lynne thought a minute. "I don't see why not," she said. "Although I do think I would keep his phone number when he leaves, just in case."

"I just hope I have a little free time on weekends."

"Girlfriend in Dallas?" Lynne asked, hoping her voice sounded properly casual.

"Nope, fishing boat in Port Isabel," Joe said. "I just have a small one now, but I can catch fish in it just as well as I can in a big one."

"Bobby López has the best bait in town," Lynne volunteered.

"Yes, I know." Joe looked up, a little surprised. "You fish too?"

Lynne nodded. "I'm not a fanatic and I absolutely *refuse* to lie about the one that got away, but, yes, I have been known to go fishing." She drained her glass of tea and set it on the porch. "I guess I'd better be going. It's almost ten and I have to be up early in the morning."

"Yeah, this place gets rolling pretty early too. You know, the only time I miss my life back in Dallas is when that alarm goes off at five-thirty. In Dallas I didn't have to get up until seven or so." He stood up and offered his hand to Lynne, who grasped it gratefully as she stood up, her high-heeled boots making her legs seem to go on forever.

Joe grasped her upper arm lightly as he walked with her toward her car. Lynne glanced down at the unexpected courtesy, her arm tingling a little at the gentle touch of his fingers on her skin. "Thanks for the tea and the conversation," she said, getting out her keys. "I wish you the best of luck with the ranch."

"Thanks, I need all the luck I can get. And thank you for bringing those papers out to Carlos. He's a hard worker, even if he doesn't always know what he's doing, and I suspect his sister is all right too."

"I hope they'll do it right this time and get her over legally," Lynne said, laughing at Joe's description of Carlos. She unlocked the door of the Fiero.

Joe peered down into the shiny new sports car. "Can you fit in there all right?" he asked, blushing to the roots of his hair when he realized what he had asked.

Lynne laughed a little self-consciously. "Yes, but I had

36

to shop around a little before I found a sports car that was comfortable." She eased her long legs into the car. "See? I do fit in here."

Joe blushed again. "I wish I had that problem," he said, more to himself than to her. "Thanks again, and I'll call you if we get any more suspicious characters around here."

Lynne laughed. "You do that. 'Night." She wheeled her car around and took the dirt road that would lead her back to the highway.

Joe stood where she had left him, watching as her tail-lights turned onto the main highway. She was a nice person, he thought as her car disappeared into the night. She had made another trip out here, even though she hadn't been obliged to, and then she had sat down and filled out those forms for Carlos. Not many border patrol agents would have done something like that.

As Joe walked back toward the house, he wished he had gotten her telephone number. They could have gone fishing together. He had been about to ask, but then she had stood up beside him and he had lost his nerve. She was so *tall!* She had towered over him a good four or five inches. Of course, two or three of those inches belonged to those boots of hers, but part of it was her long legs. Joe sighed as he sat down on the front porch. It was silly and he knew it, but tall women had always intimidated him a little, even though he had dated a couple in the past. He wondered if she was sensitive about her height. She might have been, but the fact that she had been wearing boots made him think that she wasn't. And she probably had a tall, long-legged boyfriend somewhere whom she could dance with without looking silly.

Lynne drove the speed limit down the highway that led back into Brownsville. He was just as nice on the inside as he was on the outside, she thought as she speeded up and passed a slow-moving pickup truck. When he had asked her in for a glass of tea, she had half expected him to be at least a little bit conceited, but Joe Stockton was one of the most down-to-earth people she had talked with in a long time. Either he was not conscious of his good looks or he was not impressed by them. And if his two cryptic comments were anything to go by, he was as self-conscious about being short as she was about not being very pretty.

She should have worn her tennis shoes instead of her favorite boots, but how could she have known she was going to be meeting up with Joe again tonight? She had expected that he would be in town on a date, and she had never dreamed that he would ask her to have iced tea with him. *But he still didn't see me as a woman,* she thought sadly as she drove through the outskirts of town. Even though he had been warm and fun and friendly, there were none of the visual or verbal signals from Joe that indicated any kind of sexual awareness on his part. She was sure that his taking her arm had been common courtesy, nothing more. Although Lynne's behavior had given nothing away, she had been acutely aware of Joe as an attractive man from the moment she had laid eyes on him this morning, and it hurt more than a little that he had not felt the same way about her.

Lynne drove up to her apartment, the scowl on her face brightening when she saw the old white Corvette parked in front of her place. Laura had come by to see her! Bringing the Fiero to a screeching halt, she jumped over a four-foot retaining wall and ran up the steps.

Laura was waiting on the top step, smiling down at her exuberant little sister. "I remember the good old days when I could take a fence or a wall like that," she recalled with a laugh. Lynne reached out and hugged her. Both Kosler sisters had been known for their ability to jump over hurdles on the track team.

"You will be able to again, once the baby comes."

Laura patted her slightly bulging tummy. "But that won't be for months yet," she complained. "And Dr. Rivas said pregnant women are only supposed to do mild exercise."

"Oh, Laura, I think you'll survive without jumping over the fence for the next few months." Lynne laughed. She kicked off her boots and left them in the middle of the floor. "So what brings you out to see me this late? Did you have to wait long?"

"No, as a matter of fact I just got here," Laura said, seating herself on the couch. "I came for several reasons. First, I got a letter from Mother today and knew you would want to read it."

"Can I get you something to drink?" Lynne asked.

"Sprite, if you have it," Laura said. "Where have you been?"

"I drove out to the Stockton ranch and took one of the workers a set of immigration papers for his sister. I had to take her in this morning, and I felt sorry for her." She sat down in the chair across from the couch and stretched her long legs out in front of her.

"You would." Laura smiled gently at Lynne. "That was nice. Tell me, is that nephew as good looking as they say he is?"

Lynne nodded. "Better. But he doesn't know much about ranching."

"Did you get in any flirting?" Laura asked.

Lynne blushed and shook her head. "We drank a glass of tea, but no, I didn't get in any flirting."

Laura pressed her lips together and started to say something, but Lynne took the letter from her and started to read. Their mother would write Lynne one week and Laura the next, knowing that the sisters always shared her letters to them.

Lynne scanned the letter and looked up with a frown of concern on her face. "Dennis isn't any better than he was the last time mother wrote," she said quietly. She handed the letter back to Laura.

"I know. But there weren't any guarantees when they moved out there that it was going to help much. You know, I can't help but worry that this one will inherit something like that."

"Oh, Laura, don't worry about that," Lynne reassured her. "You and Tony never had a problem like that, and neither does Laurina. Mother once said she had some asthma as a child. Besides," she said, winking, "all those good south-of-the-border genes your kids carry will protect them from that." Laura had married into a wealthy Mexican family that lived on both sides of the border, and her husband, Tony, and daughter, Laurina, held dual citizenship.

"Oh, that reminds me—the second reason I came over was to get a little practice on my Spanish before Mrs. Carvajal comes to see us next week. I always feel like such a fool—I can't talk to her and she can't talk to me."

Lynne rolled her eyes in mock exasperation. "Good grief, why practice with me? My accent's horrible. Just last week a wetback laughed in my face. Why not practice with Tony?"

40

"Because he laughs more than your wetbacks do. Please, at least you know the words, even if you can't say them right."

"Bueno," Lynne replied. *"Como está usted?"*

"Huh?" Laura asked.

"COmo esTÁ usTED," Lynne repeated slowly. "You know—how are you?"

"Is this a morning question?" Laura asked. Lynne nodded. "Then how do you say really lousy?"

"Muy malo," Lynne said. Laura repeated the phrase after Lynne, and Lynne went on to a little more conversation. As she drilled Laura in some basic conversational Spanish, she had a chance to admire her older sister. Laura was not pretty in a conventional sense, with the same long face that Lynne had, but Laura's nose was not excessively long and was perfectly straight and her lips were full and hinted of sensuality. Laura was nearly as tall as Lynne, but she had smaller bones and she had curves where Lynne had angles. Her eyes were a bright shade of green and tilted ever so slightly, giving her an exotic air, and natural blond curls cascaded down her back. Lynne had always admired her older sister, and had always accepted without the least bit of jealousy the fact that Laura was prettier. At least, she always had until tonight.

Lynne drilled Laura on her Spanish for more than an hour, helping her with phrases that would cover conversation about the house, Tony and Laurina, and Laura's job as a real estate agent. It was nearly midnight before Laura left, promising to have Lynne over one night while Mrs. Carvajal was visiting. Lynne, who dearly loved Laura's diminutive mother-in-law, assured her that she looked forward to the invitation.

Lynne stood at the window, her eyes watching Laura as she walked to her car. For the first time in years Lynne felt a little jealous of Laura. She wasn't jealous of the fact that Laura was married and had a family. Lynne had been engaged once and had broken it off herself, choosing not to marry a man she didn't really love. Nor did she begrudge Laura the Carvajal money, since the border patrol certainly paid her well enough. But she admitted to herself that she did envy Laura her looks.

Lynne sighed as she turned off the porch light. She wandered into the bathroom and stared at her face in the mirror while washing off the makeup. It didn't much matter—with the paintpots or without them she wasn't much to look at.

Lynne stripped and put on a short cotton nightgown. As she pulled back the covers and climbed in to bed, her mind drifted to Joe's handsome face and that shock of blond hair that framed it. Why couldn't she have looked like Laura? A single tear slipped down her cheek. Joe wouldn't have looked at Laura with those unseeing eyes. He would have noticed that Laura was a woman!

CHAPTER THREE

Lynne shut the door of the detention center behind her and trudged tiredly to her car. She wished somebody else had been around to process that bunch of jerks! Not only had the carload of men been illegal aliens, but they had all been slightly inebriated, and it had taken Lynne nearly two hours to process them all. Lynne crawled into the still-hot car and switched on the engine, turning the air-conditioner up full blast. If May was already this hot, what was the summer going to be like?

Lynne glanced over at the workout bag on the seat beside her and made a face. She was tempted to skip her workout and go on home, but this was her regular day and she hated to miss it, even though it was eight P.M. She had been sitting in a patrol car all day listening to the virtues of Drew's latest girlfriend, and both her mind and her body were in need of vigorous physical activity. Turning left instead of right, she drove toward the health club and parked her car next to the building. The health club catered to all age groups and was coed, except for the locker rooms and saunas, and Lynne and the other women who used the club worked out right alongside the men. Lynne enjoyed the vigorous physical activity, pushing herself to the limit on the machines.

As Lynne got out of the car, she heard the sound of another car pulling up beside hers, but she didn't look up as she reached in and pulled out her bag. It was only after she'd stepped back and bumped against a low-slung sports car that she turned around and met a pair of bright-blue eyes—Joe Stockton, just getting out of his Trans Am. Lynne's eyes widened as she stared down into his smiling face, and she felt herself take an involuntary breath at the strong feelings of response she had to him. Joe was just as attractive, just as sexy, as he had been the first time she'd seen him three weeks ago, and her awareness of him had increased since their first meeting. She nodded her head and smiled shyly. "Hello, Joe," she said softly. "How's the ranch coming along?"

"Fine, just fine," Joe said. "I even managed to deliver a calf last week. Took me longer than it did you, but I got him here safe and sound. All by myself. And how about you? Have you had time to go out riding Betsy?"

He remembered! Lynne thought with pleasure. "As a matter of fact, Betsy and I went for a long ride last Sunday afternoon," Lynne answered as Joe came around the car. "Tony and I had a great time."

"Boyfriend?" Joe asked casually.

Lynne shook her head, surprised that Joe cared who Tony was. "No, he's my brother-in-law. We took my niece riding, since my sister's expecting and isn't supposed to ride. How about you? Did you get in any fishing last weekend?"

Joe nodded his head. "Did pretty well, but it was sure lonely on that boat. Wish I'd had a little feminine companionship." He grinned and winked at her.

Lynne blushed at Joe's remark. "I wish you had too,"

44

she said with just the right amount of provocation in her voice. My goodness, was that *her* talking like that?

"Yes, it would have been great to have had a nice, warm hand to hold as that big ball of sun sank down in the sky," Joe went on, his voice rasping a little in his throat. "Somebody to share a drink with while the sun dipped lower on the horizon."

Lynne's eyes twinkled. "Don't you mean somebody to gaze at in the dusk while she helped you clean all those big, beautiful fish?" Her eyes lost their provocative look and fairly sparkled as Joe laughed out loud.

"All right, all right, that too." He grinned, taking her arm and starting toward the door of the health club. "Have you rounded up lots of aliens since I saw you last?"

Lynne nodded. "I finished processing a bunch just a few minutes ago. I think they had had a few before they came over to give them a little Dutch courage. They weren't out-and-out drunk, but it took forever to process them and one of them kept singing *'Un Poquito Más'* to me while I tried to fill out his papers."

Joe laughed out loud. "Maybe he was trying to charm you into letting him stay."

Lynne grinned impishly. "I thought that, too, until he started singing it to my supervisor. Normally, Ben's enough to scare the bats out of a cave! Needless to say, Ben was not amused." She pushed open the door of the health club and went in, showing her membership card to the young woman on duty.

Joe showed the woman his card and followed Lynne through the doors that led to the exercise floor of the club. The main exercise floor had a mixture of free weights and exercise machines, and in a room off to one

45

side a continuous aerobics class was in progress. Joe glanced through the doors at the group of mostly women who were bouncing and twisting along with the tiny instructor. "I guess you're into aerobics?" he asked.

Lynne shook her head. "I pump iron," she said, her eyes scanning the room. "But I run through the routine fairly quickly so that I get some cardiovascular good out of it."

"Good," Joe replied. Lynne looked at him questioningly and he grinned. "I can hardly wait to see those long legs in action!" He smiled wickedly as he sauntered toward the men's dressing room.

Lynne stared after him with her mouth hanging open a little. Joe had actually flirted with her! He had made those little comments about being on the boat and then he had wanted to see her legs. Well, she hoped he liked them. She hurried toward the women's locker room, as pleased by his comments as a schoolgirl. Maybe he might ask her out for a drink afterward. Lynne knew that a lot of people used the club as a singles bar, and she had made a few dates here herself. Did she dare hope that maybe Joe was interested?

Lynne pulled on her T-shirt and jogging shorts. Most of the women in the club wore leotards and tights, but Lynne felt freer to move in the shorts and T-shirt. She stepped on the scale and stuck out her tongue. One hundred and fifty pounds on six feet wasn't all that thin, but on her it looked it. She looked down at the long, thin legs that Joe had wanted to see and some of her earlier exuberance faded. She made a face, hoping he wouldn't be too disappointed. For the first time since she had joined the club, Lynne was self-conscious walking out on the

46

exercise floor, as she met Joe's eyes from one of the exercise bicycles.

Joe grinned and winked at Lynne, his eyes making an inspection of her figure. They traveled the length of her body as hers traveled the length of his, his eyes taking in the long, angular lines of her arms, the firm uptilt of her high breasts. His eyes drifted lower, past the narrow, flat waist and boyish hips to those long legs that seemed to go on forever. Although she was not shapely in the traditional sense, for the first time Joe could sense the vulnerable femininity that most of the time Lynne kept hidden from the world, and he wondered for a minute what it would be like to hold her in his arms. Would she be soft and warm to hold?

Lynne returned Joe's inspection, first gazing at the well-formed legs usually concealed by Joe's work clothes. Then she moved up to his chest, tonight hidden under his T-shirt, and remembered what it had looked like the night they had shared iced tea. He would look beautiful in the nude, she thought, blushing again as she pictured him, proud and masculine. Shaking her head to rid herself of these thoughts, she crossed the floor and took the only other empty exercise bicycle, right next to Joe's. She moved the tension lever to a fairly high setting, and when she had set her rhythm, she glanced over at Joe, who was beginning to breathe a little raggedly. "Been on the bike long?" she asked.

Joe shook his head as he reached down and lessened the tension on his bicycle. "No, I had just gotten on when you came out." He stared down pointedly at her legs. "I knew they'd be gorgeous," he said, and returned his attention to his pedaling.

Lynne blushed prettily as she pumped away. She knew

47

her legs were not gorgeous, but it was sweet of him to say they were. By the end of ten-minute warm-up exercise both she and Joe were breathing hard and just beginning to sweat. They climbed off the bicycles together and walked across to the exercise machines. "Are you sure it's all right for you to use these?" Joe asked doubtfully. "Won't you hurt yourself or something?"

Lynne hoisted a slant-board to the highest setting on the stand. "Of course not," she scoffed. "I've been doing it for more than a year." She lay down on the slant-board and proceeded to count out fifty sit-ups.

Joe adjusted the slant-board next to hers one notch down from the top and proceeded to do sit-ups along with Lynne, although Lynne could tell he was slowing down once they had gone over thirty. *How does she do it?* Joe wondered. He ignored the muscles in his stomach that were screaming in protest and fought to keep up with Lynne's brisk pace.

Lynne kept up her steady pace until she had reached the fifty mark. She sat up and stared at Joe, who was struggling to pull himself up. When he saw that she was staring at him, he grinned and stayed in the sitting position. "Finished?" he asked.

"Yes, but you go ahead and finish," Lynne said. She whirled around and held the ankle restrainers with her hands.

"Uh, I think I've done enough," Joe said, and turned around and positioned himself as she was. Rhythmically, they raised and lowered their legs in time with the rock music that was blaring out of the speakers. It was nice to have somebody to work out with, Joe thought, watching Lynne's long legs pump up and down beside his own. They counted out fifty lifts together and rolled off the boards. "I guess we're going to have to share the rest of the machines," he said. "You can go first."

Lynne smiled and adjusted the weight on the leg press machine to her usual two hundred twenty-five pounds, not seeing the look of surprise on Joe's face when she sat down and almost effortlessly pushed the weights back and forth. She pressed her usual count and hopped off the machine. "Your turn," she said brightly.

Joe removed twenty pounds from the stack of weights. He sat down and pushed at the weights for a minute before he gave up and took ten more pounds off the stack. Lynne watched Joe push the weights back and forth. The muscles in his neck were tight and it was obvious that he was working a lot to pump that much.

Lynne set the military press to seventy-five pounds and started pumping. Joe finished with the leg press machine and stood beside the military press while Lynne pushed the handles high above her head. "You're pretty good," he said as Lynne raised and lowered the bar for the last time.

"Thanks," she mumbled. She got off the machine and turned to the next one, a machine that duplicated the motion of rowing. She glanced over at the military press and noticed that Joe had added only ten pounds to her weights. She was embarrassed, since she had thought that men were supposed to be able to pump about twice what a woman could on that one. She did her repetitions on the rowing machine and went to the arm curls, which she had never been any good at. She noticed that Joe was using the same setting on the rowing machine as she had, and he shrugged as his embarrassed eyes met hers.

Good Lord, she must think I'm the biggest wimp in Brownsville! he thought.

49

Lynne left the arm-curl machine and got on the Roman chair. At least he was better at that one than she was! He increased the setting on the arm-curl by three notches and lifted the bar rhythmically as Lynne's lanky body arced up and down on the machine. And even though she was taller than he, he must have outweighed her a good twenty or thirty pounds. She sure didn't look that strong!

Lynne relinquished the Roman chair and adjusted another of the leg machines to a high setting, this one designed to exercise the muscles in the back of the legs. Well, so much for his asking her out tonight, Lynne thought sadly as she pumped her legs up and down. Joe looked as embarrassed by his lack of muscle strength as she was by the fact that she was stronger than he. Why couldn't she have gone to the aerobics class instead of coming out here and unwittingly making a fool of him on the exercise floor? She knew she was stronger than most of the women and a lot of the men who used the machines, but she would never have guessed by looking at Joe that he was one of them. He looked as though he were in better shape than that!

With her eyes lowered and her face burning, Lynne suffered through the rest of her workout. She did not reduce the weights that she normally used, since it was pointless by now to try to pretend that she was weaker than she really was. She finished with the last machine she used and mumbled a good-night to Joe, then hurried toward the women's dressing room.

Joe stared after Lynne with puzzlement in his eyes. Why, she was more embarrassed than he had been! Sure, he had felt a little silly at first, not being as strong as she was, but it didn't bother him all that much. She looked as though she could have fallen through a crack in the floor. As the door of the dressing room banged shut, Joe realized that she thought she had embarrassed him. He shook his head. Lynne Kosler was a strange one, all right, but he liked her, and she intrigued him more than any woman he'd met in a long time. Well, tonight he wasn't going to be intimidated by those long legs of hers, he promised himself. He skipped his last two machines and hurried to the men's dressing room.

You really blew it, Lynne, she told herself in disgust as she stripped the sweaty exercise clothes from her body and threw them into the exercise bag along with her crumpled uniform. The most attractive man she had ever met in her life starts to come on to her a little, and she has to embarrass him by showing off her superior strength. Where had she been when they were handing out the feminine wiles? Right behind the door, same place she had been standing when they handed out the beauty!

A few minutes later Lynne had showered, dressed in a pair of designer jeans and a soft shirt, and pinned up her hair in a wet knot on the back of her head. She dabbed on a little lipstick and eye shadow, but figured she didn't need any more makeup than that to walk through the lobby of the health club. She was still sorry that she had blown her chance of going out with Joe, but by now she was feeling a little more philosophical about the incident. He probably wouldn't have asked her out anyway. A little flirting didn't mean anything. Men did it all the time. Now, where could she pick up a quick late supper on the way home?

Debating the merits of a pizza over a couple of tacos, Lynne didn't see the figure lounging beside the door or

51

hear his voice call her name until he moved directly into her path. "Joe!" she exclaimed as she bumped up against him. "I didn't see you. I'm sorry." She blushed; Joe's hand had brushed against the side of her breast.

"It's all right. I figured the only way I could get your attention was to let you mow me down," he teased, his blue eyes twinkling. "What on earth had you so preoccupied? I called your name twice."

"Supper," Lynne said. "I haven't eaten yet. I was trying to decide between tacos and pizza."

"Hmm. I was planning to ask you out for a drink, but now I guess it will have to be for a whole meal," Joe said honestly. "Where would you like to go?"

"Uh, no, that's all right. No, I mean, I'd love to go out for a drink, but you don't have to feed me supper," Lynne stammered.

"Don't be ridiculous. Besides, if you faint from hunger, I'm not going to be able to pick you up. You ought to know that after tonight!" Lynne blushed and Joe laughed. "Hey, come on. Let me feed you and get to know you a little better. How about it?"

Lynne smiled shyly. "Have you eaten yet?"

"Yes, but I can always have a snack while you eat."

"There's a little place right on the other side of the border that makes the best chili rellenos and tequila sunrises that you ever tasted," she said.

"Maxie's?" Joe asked.

Lynne nodded eagerly. "How about it? Are you game?"

"Sure, what's a little heartburn tomorrow? Come on, we'll take my car." Joe took Lynne by the hand and led her from the health club.

Lynne got into the Trans Am with Joe. "Which bridge is Maxie's closer to?" he asked.

"The new bridge," Lynne said, referring to the newer of the two bridges that would take them into Matamoros. Joe drove through downtown Brownsville, to the large grocery-store parking lot where, for a fee, Joe could park his car while they went across the border. They locked the Trans Am, and Joe took Lynne's hand. They walked up to the toll bridge that would take them into Mexico and strolled across stopping for a minute to stare down into the waters of the Rio Grande, the moonlight making the usually murky water sparkle. Was the night beautiful, Lynne asked herself, or was it just that she was with Joe?

Joe sniffed the air as they stepped off the bridge. "Is it my imagination, or does the air smell different over here?" he asked.

"Well, in this part of town it's your imagination," Lynne said dryly. Joe laughed, knowing what she meant. They looked around for a minute at the small plaza lined with taxies that greeted visitors to Matamoros. Lights twinkled from the streetlights and from the shops and cafés that surrounded the plaza. "Have you come over to the market?" Lynne asked. The market was a taxi ride away and sold everything from touristy junk to fine leather and silver work.

"I brought my mother last weekend," Joe said. "She bought up a bunch of those Mexican dresses for her friends in Dallas. You like those?"

"When I can find one long enough," Lynne admitted. "I have a couple."

"That's not Mom's problem," Joe said cheerfully. "She has to take all hers up."

"Lucky Mom," Lynne said. "It's a pain trying to find

53

clothes to fit. I usually end up paying Maria, my seamstress, to make them for me. Of course, that way I end up with originals at a fraction of the price I'd have to pay in the store."

"And you probably look like a million dollars in them," Joe said warmly. His comment made Lynne glow with pleasure. Even if it really wasn't true, it was nice of Joe to say those things. "So, Lynne, do we want to walk or do we take a taxi?"

"Are you up to walking? It's just a couple of blocks over and the street's lighted all the way," she said.

Joe took her elbow and they started down the street that was lined with small shops and bars and hotels. They strolled slowly, peering into the windows of the shops and making imaginary purchases of gold and silver and primitive artwork. She was one of the most enjoyable women he had met in a long time, Joe thought as Lynne roared with laughter at a drawing of Elvis Presley on velvet and threatened to buy it for his living room. Most of his girlfriends in Dallas would have been bored stiff by window-shopping down here, but she was having a ball.

Maxie's was a small place, a little dingy on the outside, but the interior was warm and cozy. The bar-cum-restaurant was crowded, but they spotted a newly vacated table across the room and made a beeline for it. The waitress, who was trying to clear the table, scowled a little at them until Joe flashed her his winning smile, at which point she broke into a beaming smile herself and brought the menus. Lynne grinned across the table at Joe. "Flash that smile and a little of that sex appeal and you having them jumping to do your bidding," she teased.

Joe grinned sheepishly. "It just comes naturally," he

admitted. "I'm not consciously trying to manipulate women, honestly I'm not."

"I know that," Lynne said softly. She didn't know Joe all that well, but from what she did know, she believed that he wouldn't consciously use his good looks or his sex appeal to get his way with a woman. But he did use it unconsciously, as all attractive men, and women, did.

"Order anything you want," Joe said.

"Anything?" Her stomach growled loud enough for Joe to hear it across the table.

Joe laughed. "Yes, anything. I still owe you one for delivering that calf last month, and from the sound of your stomach, you need to be fed! How about the house special with a side order of chili rellenos?"

Lynne nodded eagerly. "You bet. Better catch the waitress before she goes off."

Joe flashed the waitress another of his bright smiles and she scurried back to their table. "Lynne would like the house special and a side order of chili rellenos. What do you want to drink?"

"I'll have a tequila sunrise," Lynne said.

"And I'll have an order of chili rellenos and a Perrier," Joe said. They handed the waitress their menus.

Lynne looked across the table at Joe. "You don't drink?" she asked. She was surprised. From what she had heard about Joe's life-style, she wouldn't have put him down as a teetotaler.

Joe nodded his head. "That's off my diet."

"The chili rellenos aren't going to do your calorie count that much good either," she reminded him.

Joe shook his head. "It isn't that kind of diet. I'm diabetic. It's the alcohol I can't have."

"You are?" Lynne said. Her face softened in sympathy. "Oh, I'm so sorry. Have you had it long?"

Joe shook his head even as he smiled at her concern. "Don't be sorry," he told her. "It's no big deal, I can promise you that. I've had it since I was a kid, and as long as I take my insulin shot in the morning and don't take in too many calories and don't skip meals, I can live a completely normal life. Completely normal," he repeated in a sexy whisper, raising one eyebrow suggestively.

"Oh, that's a relief!" Lynne cried. "I wouldn't have wanted the women of Dallas to feel deprived."

Joe broke out in whoops of laughter. "Lynne, you're something else," he said when he could control his laughing long enough. "And I want to assure you that the ladies of Dallas had nothing to complain about."

Lynne looked him up and down. "Glad to hear it."

The waitress served their drinks. Lynne took a sip of hers.

"But seriously, other than not hurting your sex life"— Lynne blushed here a little—"does it restrict you in any way? Is that why you can't pump as much as I can?"

Joe shook his head and sipped his drink. "Heavens, no. Diabetes doesn't affect muscle strength. There are a number of amateur and professional athletes who are diabetic. In fact, I was on the swim team in college. No, I'm afraid I have to attribute my lack of strength to pushing a pencil in a Dallas bank for six years. I kept my weight down because of the diabetes but otherwise didn't keep in shape, and now I'm paying the price. That first month on the ranch nearly killed me."

"I can imagine," Lynne murmured. "What did you do for the bank?"

"Oh, a lot of things. By the time I left, I was a loan officer and was bucking for a promotion to vice-president. Would have made it, too, if I hadn't inherited the ranch."

The waitress placed a huge, steaming plate in front of Lynne and a smaller plate with the chili rellenos to one side. She put Joe's chili rellenos in front of him and Joe asked for another Perrier for himself and one for Lynne. "Is that all right?" he asked. "That stuff might burn your mouth."

Lynne nodded and sampled a chili relleno, gasping with pained pleasure as she bit into the spicy concoction. She fanned her mouth and grabbed Joe's Perrier and drank several swallows of it. "Sorry, that was hot." She paused a minute to let the tears clear from her eyes. "Did you like your work in the bank?"

Joe shrugged. "It was a living," he said. "And Dallas is great if you're young and single." He flashed her a genuine smile. "But I like it better down here, even if I still have to learn how to run that place. In fact, that's why I started working out. I'm going to have to be in shape to do the work out there." He sampled a chili relleno and reclaimed his Perrier. "And how about you—do you lift weights to keep in shape for your job?"

"That's not why I started, but it helps," Lynne admitted, taking a bite of the spicy guacamole.

"Why did you start?" Joe asked. "Boyfriend into it?"

Lynne shook her head. "No, I started because I thought if I lifted weights, I might not be so thin looking. It hasn't done any good that way, but the strength and the stamina do help on the job."

Joe leaned out from the table and looked up and down Lynne's slender body. "You look all right to me," he said. "So when do you need the extra strength on your job?"

"It helps a lot of the time," Lynne said. "Like when we're tracking aliens through the pasture. Sometimes we go ten or twelve hours before we catch them."

"Is it hard to track?" Joe asked.

"Sometimes it can be a challenge," Lynne admitted. "You have to be able to spot little things—a broken twig, a rock out of place—that indicate that a human's come through recently. It takes a special knack."

"And you have that knack," Joe said perceptively.

The waitress brought the fresh Perriers, and Lynne and Joe each grabbed one and drank gratefully.

Lynne nodded. "And then it's nice to be able to get out of the way when the bullets start flying."

"Bullets!" Joe said, his head snapping up. "You mean you get *shot at?*"

"Sure. I don't wear a thirty-eight for fun, Joe. It doesn't happen all that often, but just last year, Bill Jackson and I were on a night stakeout in a pasture near the river where we had heard a crossing was to be made. The leader opened fire on us when we tried to round them up. I spent most of that night flat on the ground behind a rotted log. But we tracked them most of the next day, and that bastard's behind bars now."

"Is that the only time you've ever been shot at?" Joe asked anxiously.

"Well, it happened once the first year I was on the force, but it was just one wild shot. And then, just last winter, Bert and I were down in a ditch on a highway stakeout when we were scared half to death." Lynne started laughing at the memory.

"I'm almost scared to hear this one," Joe said. "It must be a real doozy."

"Oh, it is." Lynne giggled. "It was cold that night, and

58

Bert's wife had made us up a big Thermos of coffee. Bert and I were down in the ditch and the Thermos was sitting between us, where we thought it was just out of sight. Well, lo and behold, this big old pickup pulls up and somebody gets out and picks off that Thermos, clean as a whistle. Well, Bert and I come up out of there, our pistols cocked and ready, and find two Anglos standing there, scared out of their wits. Dad's out teaching junior to shoot, and they thought the gleam off that Thermos in the moonlight was a rabbit's eyes. I'm not sure who was more scared there for a minute—them or us."

Joe laughed out loud. "Was the man in any trouble?"

Lynne shook her head. "No, and the next afternoon he came around with the biggest, prettiest Thermos you ever saw! I've never seen a man so apologetic."

"It sounds like you get your share of excitement," Joe commented. As they finished their meal, Lynne talked a little more about her work, describing the drudgery and the frustration of the job as well as the exciting parts, and said that until Americans stopped hiring illegal aliens, she and her fellow agents were fighting a losing battle. Joe shared some of his hopes and dreams for his new ranch, and told her about his family in Dallas. She found out that his father was an attorney and his mother did volunteer work.

It was late by the time Joe finally asked for the check. He and Lynne spent the better part of two hours just talking and laughing together, and he couldn't remember when he had enjoyed an impromptu date more. He took her hand on their way out of the small cantina. "That was fun," he said as they strolled back down the street toward the bridge. "We'll have to do it again. Only, next time we'll eat early and I'll eat with you."

"That would be nice," Lynne said quietly, a ripple of pleasure passing through her body. He wanted to see her again! He wasn't handing her a line—she had been handed enough of those in her lifetime to know when a man meant that he would see her again and when he didn't. And Joe definitely intended to see her again.

But as a buddy or as a woman? Lynne glanced over at the man by her side. He had worn tennis shoes again, so in her boots she towered over him. Maybe he just wanted a friend, the friend most men wanted her to be. And if he just wanted her to be his buddy and listen to his tales of woe about his girlfriends, she wasn't sure she was up to that, as strong as her physical attraction to him was. Still, he had flirted with her and had complimented her several times this evening, so maybe he thought she was a little bit appealing. Well, if he kissed her good-night she would know. She squeezed Joe's hand, and he squeezed hers back before letting go of it and settling his arm around her waist.

She does feel soft against me, Joe thought as they walked slowly across the bridge. He and Lynne were the only pedestrians on it, and Joe smiled in the darkness as she wrapped her arm around his waist. He couldn't believe the strong sensual pull he felt toward this woman. She wasn't his usual type, that was for sure, yet he wanted to kiss her and touch her tonight. He wanted to see her in her shorts again. He wanted to see her small breasts unconfined and feel them grow hard in his hand. She wasn't pretty, not like the women he had known in Dallas, and she didn't have the fashionable flair that might have made her striking, but she still appealed to him, and much to his surprise, not just as a friend. She appealed to him as a woman, a very sexy woman.

They reached the American side of the border and showed their driver's licenses. Lynne spoke to the customs agent on duty and commiserated with him for having drawn such a boring shift, and together she and Joe walked back to where the Trans Am was parked. Joe's grip tightened on her waist and Lynne held her breath. She was ready for his kiss, and so was disappointed when Joe released his hold to unlock the door of the car. "I'll take you back to the health club to pick up your car," he said, opening the door and holding it for her.

Well, now you know, she thought disappointedly as Joe drove them back toward the health club. He just wanted her for a buddy. He didn't want to kiss her as she wanted to kiss him. She quickly blinked back tears of disappointment. Joe pulled into the parking lot of the health club, and before he had killed the engine Lynne was out of the car. "Thanks for dinner and drinks," she said as she unlocked the door of the Fiero.

Damn, she was about to get away before he could kiss her. Joe hopped out of the Trans Am. He walked up to where Lynne was standing and whirled her around to face him. "Hey, woman, don't I get a good-night kiss?"

Lynne lit up like a Christmas tree. "Oh, yes," she breathed, and smiled down into Joe's handsome face.

Joe looked up into her glowing eyes for a minute. He started to raise his lips to hers, but shook his head and took Lynne's shoulders and gently pushed her into a sitting position on the hood of the Trans Am before insinuating himself between her knees, bending his head, and taking sweet possession of her mouth.

Lynne's lips opened to Joe's like flower petals in the sun. He touched her lips lightly once, twice, before crushing her to him and kissing her hungrily, deeply, giving vent to the strong attraction he felt. She opened her lips to Joe and curled her arms up around his neck, savoring the way his soft blond hair felt in her hands as she ran her fingers through it. *This feels so sweet,* she thought as Joe slid his arms around her waist and pressed her close to his hard, warm body. The musky scent of his aftershave tantalized her nostrils. She let her hands glide down his shoulders to his broad chest, and she cursed the barrier of his shirt as she pictured the soft blond hair that covered his chest and stomach. She wanted to touch him, to feel his skin next to hers. Joe pressed himself to her, and she snuggled as close to him as she could, her soft breasts pressed against the hard wall of his chest. She could feel her nipples swell with passion for Joe, and she could feel the strength of his passion for her as he tightened the grip he had on her waist.

She was soft and warm as a kitten, Joe thought, pulling Lynne's warm, willing body closer to his. But he could feel the hardened tips of her breasts against his chest, and he knew that she was as affected by their embrace as he was. He offered his tongue and immediately felt it being met by hers. Thrusting, feinting, they played back and forth, their arousal growing by the second as they kissed and touched and caressed one another in the darkness of the parking lot. Joe lightly stroked the skin of her thigh where his leg touched hers. Finally, both knowing they were playing with fire, they eased out of their torrid embrace. "You're some sexy lady, but I guess you already know that," Joe breathed as he placed light, caressing kisses down Lynne's brow.

Lynne shook her head. "No more so than you," she answered, touching the outside of one of Joe's thighs. She felt the tension in him and then they were kissing again, drawn together for another searing embrace, this one even more torrid than the last.

Finally Joe tore his mouth from hers and moved away from Lynne. "We keep this up and we're going to be making love in one of these little bitty cars," he said. He thrust his hands in his pockets to keep from reaching for Lynne again.

Lynne nodded wordlessly. "I know. And I can think of a lot of places that would be more comfortable!" She bit her lip, realizing how forward she sounded.

Joe laughed out loud at her embarrassment. "Lynne, you're priceless," he said. "I want to see you again, and soon. Are you off this weekend?"

"I have to work Sunday, but I'm off all day Saturday," she said.

"That's great. How about going fishing with me on Saturday? We'll take a picnic out on the boat and I'll feed you a swanky dinner afterward. But only on one condition."

"What's that?" she asked.

"Wear your flats!" Joe pleaded.

Lynne laughed and nodded eagerly. "I'd love to," she assured him. Joe sat her back down and kissed her again before he let her get into the Fiero and drive away.

Lynne's lips were still tingling as she unlocked the door of her apartment and ran to the mirror in the bathroom. Had she suddenly changed from an ugly duckling into a swan? No, she was still plain old Lynne, but this plain old Lynne looked thoroughly kissed, and her eyes had a sparkle in them. Lynne reached out and pinched herself. No, she hadn't died and gone to heaven. She just felt as if she had.

Joe, pulling onto the bumpy dirt road that would take

him to his front door, whistled softly. My God, that woman could kiss! She might not be the prettiest woman who had ever been in his arms, but one kiss from her had moved him more than making love to most of the others had. Joe was surprised, really surprised, that he was so attracted to her. He had never in his life been drawn to such an ordinary-looking woman. But she was only ordinary on the outside, Joe thought as he pulled up in front of the house and killed his engine. Inside she was a real beauty!

CHAPTER FOUR

Lynne yawned as she pulled on her bikini bottoms and a pair of cutoff jeans. Sleepily she put on her swimsuit top and a T-shirt over it, and braided her hair. Making a face at the clock, which read six forty-five, she wandered into the kitchen and put on the coffee that she desperately needed if she was going to make it through a day of fishing with Joe in Port Isabel. She and Drew had spent half the night tracking a group of illegal aliens through a pasture outside Raymondville, and if it had been anyone else but Joe, she would have called this morning and begged off the fishing trip. But she had looked forward to seeing Joe again for most of the week, and she wasn't going to let lack of sleep stop her from going with him today.

Lynne had finished about a half a cup of coffee when Joe knocked on the door. She met him with a smile on her face. "How do you like your coffee?" she asked as Joe shut the door behind him.

"Straight into the veins, after the night I put in last night," Joe answered, hiding a yawn behind his hand.

"Hot date?" Lynne asked teasingly, although she hoped it hadn't been a date. She poured Joe a cup of coffee and handed it to him.

"Hot date with one of the mares in foal," Joe said. He rubbed his eyes. He sipped a little of the coffee. "I only got a couple of hours of sleep."

"You should have called," Lynne said, filling her cup. "We could have made it another time."

"No way. I've been looking forward to this all week. Got us a picnic packed?"

Lynne nodded and smiled, tickled that Joe had wanted to come even on two hours sleep. "You can take a nap later this afternoon," she suggested in the midst of another yawn.

"Hot date of your own last night?"

"Hot date with a bunch of aliens out in the pasture," Lynne said. "But I'm all right."

"Maybe you can join me for that nap." He winked at her. "I'll never tell if you snore!"

"Sleep, my foot!" Lynne said. "I'm not going to sleep. I'm going to catch all the fish while you sleep!"

Joe swallowed the rest of his coffee in one gulp. "And if we don't get out there, the fish will all be gone. Is this lunch?" He gestured to the cooler and the knapsack on the couch.

"Yes, that's lunch and my things." She picked up the knapsack and Joe carried the cooler out to the dilapidated truck she had seen the first day on the ranch.

"Forgive me for not bringing the Trans Am, but it doesn't have a trailer hitch yet," Joe said.

Lynne looked puzzled as she climbed into the cab of the truck. "Why should I have to forgive you?"

Joe got in and started the engine. "It isn't really a very classy vehicle in which to take a lady on a date," he said as he pulled out of the parking lot of her apartment building. "I think my uncle bought it the year I graduated from high school."

"Why should I mind riding in an antique truck?" Lynne teased. "I understand they're quite the rage these days."

"It's not *that* old. I graduated from high school ten years ago. My reunion's coming up this summer."

"I won't have one for a couple of years yet," Lynne volunteered.

"Really? Are you that old? I thought you were younger than that, even," Joe said. "I—I mean, you act mature but you don't look it—I mean, you don't seem that—oh, you know!" Joe stammered, and Lynne laughed out loud at him.

"Why don't you put the other foot in and chew it?" Lynne asked. "I'm twenty-six and don't mind in the least if you think I look younger than I am." It was her one advantage, and she was proud of it.

"Well, it worked against me in the bank," Joe admitted. "I finally got a pair of clear glasses and wore them just to look a little older. Sometimes being a pretty boy is a pain in the neck."

"But not all that often," Lynne mused.

Joe grinned at some memory. "No, not all that often," he agreed. He turned the corner that would put him on the road to Port Isabel. This early on Saturday morning the streets were almost deserted, and soon they were driving past the port of Brownsville, where huge ships from all over the world loaded and unloaded cargo. "There's more coffee in the Thermos on the floor if you want it," Joe hinted.

Lynne picked up the Thermos and unscrewed the lid.

67

"Mind sharing?" she asked. "You only brought one cup." She poured the cup half-full and handed it to Joe.

"It isn't as good as yours," he said, handing Lynne the steaming brew.

"It's fine," she assured him, and handed it back to him. Lynne trembled when he placed his lips over the small pink spot her lip gloss had made on the side of the cup. It was as though he were kissing her again. Joe said nothing, but there was just a hint of desire in his eyes.

They didn't say much on the drive to Port Isabel, but they shared two more cups of coffee and by the time they had reached the outskirts of the little fishing town Lynne felt considerably more wide awake, although she didn't know whether to thank the caffeine or the sensual, flirtatious looks Joe had been giving her.

Joe pulled up in front of a dry dock on the outside of town. "I store the boat here," he said, backing the truck up to one of the wide doors. "It saves me hauling it back and forth."

Lynne got out of the truck and stood waiting beside the dock. "What are you doing out of the truck?" Joe asked.

"Wouldn't you like some help?"

"Sure, I would," Joe said as he unlocked the door. He flashed Lynne a bright smile of gratitude. None of the girls he had dated in Dallas would have offered to help him hitch a boat to a trailer! He decided right then that Lynne had to be the nicest woman he had ever met.

"Hey, that's a neat boat," Lynne said, spotting the eighteen-foot Boston Whaler.

"I got a good deal on it."

They made quick work of hooking the trailer to the truck, and soon they were driving through the little fishing town, its simple charm such a contrast to the swanky, touristy hotels and restaurants across the causeway on South Padre Island. "Do you want to try your hand at bay fishing or go out some?" Joe asked.

"Either one's fine with me," Lynne said.

"Let's make it the bay, then. I'm not feeling real ambitious today, after last night."

They bought bait from Bobby López, and Joe drove to one of the public boat launches. Lynne again offered to help, and Joe was again surprised when she didn't seem to mind getting her shoes drenched and her cutoffs damp. Joe appreciated her willingness to pitch in and help, and her unselfconscious attitude pleased him. Most of the women he had known would have insisted on staying bone dry and perfectly made up for the entire day.

In just a few minutes he and Lynne were blasting out into the bay, the wind whipping Joe's hair straight back from his face and blowing Lynne's braid up a little from her neck. They went under the tall causeway bridge and past a couple of miles of hotels and restaurants on South Padre Island before they came to quiet, unspoiled beaches. Joe went a little farther up into the bay, killed his engine and put up the protective tarp that would keep them from getting roasted during their hours in the boat. "I fished here once before and did great," he said, handing Lynne a rod and reel.

"I hope we catch at least a few," Lynne said. She unfolded a lawn chair and baited her hook. "If nothing else, it will give me the first chance I've had all week to sit down and not do anything!"

"Actually, I think that's a lot of the charm of fishing," Joe admitted. He opened a second lawn chair and baited

69

his own hook. "It's a socially acceptable way to do absolutely nothing for a few hours."

"Well, not quite nothing," Lynne said—she'd just felt a tug on her rod. Seconds later she reeled in a perfectly respectable speckled trout and put him on the stringer.

Just as Lynne was settling back into her chair, Joe felt a tug on his own rod. "What was that about sitting still?" he asked, reeling in a flounder. He added it to the stringer and settled back down in his chair.

They caught fish all morning. Since neither of them was a fanatic about maintaining silence while fishing, they talked on and off, sharing a quiet, pleasant sort of companionship. The day turned warmer, and Joe shucked his shirt, leaving him dressed in only a pair of closely fitting cutoffs that clung to his hips and thighs like a second skin. Lynne sneaked peeks at Joe when he wasn't looking, admiring the muscles in his chest and his legs. Although his arms and face were darker than his body, thanks to long hours of working outside in a shirt, his chest was tanned also, the blond hair covering it a pale contrast. Lynne longed to reach out and touch and see if it was as soft as it looked.

When the sun was high in the sky, Lynne got the cooler out from under the seat. "I brought cheese sticks. Swiss or cheddar?" she asked as she got out the plates.

"Some of both," Joe said.

Lynne unwrapped the cheese sticks and put them on the plate. "Carrot sticks?"

"Please."

Lynne put the carrot sticks on his plate. "I brought sugar-free Cokes and an apple," she volunteered, and added those to his plate.

"Say, how did you know what to feed me?"

"I tried to call you and couldn't get an answer, so I called my doctor's office. His nurse helped me put together lunch."

Joe reached out and ran his hand down the side of Lynne's face. "Thanks," he said softly.

Lynne was hungry, having missed breakfast, and ate more than Joe. Afterward, they threw their crumbs into the water and watched the smaller fish gobble them down. The wind blowing across the bay was quite warm and Lynne was beginning to get hot; but she found herself too shy to take off her shorts or shirt in front of Joe, so she suffered the heat stoically. Lynne returned to her fishing, and Joe spread out a large beach towel on the hull and lay down on it. Lynne was becoming hotter by the minute, and was grateful to notice a short time later that Joe had dozed off. She could take off her cutoffs and her shirt, and fish in her bikini for a little while before Joe woke up.

She wiggled out of the jeans and pulled the shirt over her head, sighing in relief as the breeze hit the heated flesh of her midriff. She tried to fish for a half hour or so, but the morning's coffee had worn off and her late night was catching up with her. The fourth time she caught herself nodding off, she gave up, got her bait out of the water, and spread out a towel across the bench in the back of the boat. No longer intent on fighting off her sleepiness, she shut her eyes and was asleep almost instantly.

Joe blinked his eyes and checked his waterproof wristwatch. If they had eaten around noon, he had been asleep for nearly an hour. Lynne must think he was awfully boring. He turned over, expecting to find her fishing from her chair, and was surprised to find her stripped to a brief bikini and sound asleep on the bench in the back of the boat. Joe stared at the thin, soft expanse of flesh her swimsuit revealed and was very much aroused by Lynne's near nudity, and he found himself mentally filling in what little the bikini covered and liking what he saw. He would love to touch those small breasts and cover them with hot kisses, and his fingers itched to stroke the soft skin at Lynne's waist and explore the indention of her navel. And those glorious, long legs—he would love to feel them wrapped around him, holding him tightly as he possessed her. Joe's breathing became ragged; he tried to push away the mental image of making sweet, passionate love to Lynne.

Lynne's eyes flickered open and stared into Joe's. She swallowed as his eyes traveled slowly down her face and her body, stopping to dwell on her breasts for a moment before taking in her long legs. Lynne felt immediate, paralyzing shyness. She was sure she looked funny to him, after all the beautiful women he had known in Dallas. She sat up quickly and reached for her shirt. "Don't put that on," Joe said quickly. "It's too hot."

Lynne shot him a dirty look. "I feel a little silly practically naked in front of you," she said, jerking the shirt on over her head.

"Aw, and here I was admiring the view," Joe teased. He crawled off the hull of the boat and, without batting an eyelash, unzipped his cutoffs and revealed one of the briefest bikinis Lynne had ever seen on a man. He kicked his cutoffs across the boat. "Better?" he asked.

"Not really," Lynne mumbled as she took in the perfection of Joe's body and glanced down at her own.

Joe raised an eyebrow at Lynne. "Oh, come on. It's sweltering out here, and you're bound to be hot."

"Oh, all right." She pulled off her shirt. It was silly to be shy when he had already seen her in the suit.

"That's better," Joe said. "I like a little scenery. Care to swim off the side for a little while?"

"Sure," Lynne replied, holding her nose and falling backward off the boat. Joe joined her in the water, ducking her and splashing her when she came up for air.

"You know we're scaring off every fish within ten miles of here," Lynne said. She flopped onto her back and splashed Joe in the face with her feet.

"So? I think we caught enough," Joe answered, turning onto his back also, and kicking just enough to stay afloat. As Lynne paddled along beside him, she gradually got over her shyness about Joe's seeing her in a bikini. She wasn't all that modest, not really, but Joe was so good looking!

They played in the water for a long time. Joe wanted to try a new spot, and when they found that the fishing was good they spent another hour there, catching fish almost as fast as they got their bait in the water. They poured what ice was left in Lynne's cooler over the fish and rushed back to Port Isabel to buy enough ice to keep the catch fresh. "Do you want to go back to my place and cook it tonight?" Lynne asked on their way from the ice house.

"No, why don't you come out tomorrow night and I'll cook 'em for you then," Joe said. "There's a new place on South Padre Island a friend from Dallas has been raving about for the last six months, and I thought we might try it tonight."

Lynne looked down at her sunburned, salty skin and her wet clothes. "Oh, Joe, we can't go anywhere like this! We both look a mess."

Joe looked down at his own damp, fishy-smelling clothes. "I guess you're right."

Lynne sighed in relief.

"You brought a change of clothes, didn't you?" Joe said suddenly. "Why don't you change in the lady's room? I have something I could put on."

Lynne looked down at herself in dismay. Even with a change of clothes she would still look bad. "I can't go home and change?"

Joe checked his watch. "It's after six now. If we drive back to Brownsville and then back here, it will be nearly nine before we can eat. I can't wait that long, Lynne. I have to eat around six or seven. If we don't eat now, we'll have to eat the minute we get back to Brownsville."

"That's right," she said quietly. "I forgot about that."

"Lynne, they'll let us use the restrooms here to change," Joe said. "Don't worry. You'll look fine." He kissed her cheek lightly. "How about it, Lynne?"

What could she say? "Sure, we can change here," Lynne said. She bit her lip. "Just don't expect any miracles, all right?"

Lynne took her knapsack and her purse into the bathroom. Why, oh, why had she let Joe talk her into this? Her nose was bright red and her hair was a sticky, salty mess. She jerked the rubber band out of her hair and stripped off her wet clothes, putting her shirt into the sink and soaking it. She wiped the salt from her body as best she could with the shirt and held her head under the cold water tap, trying to rinse some of the salt from her hair. Cursing herself for not having brought her makeup, she dried herself quickly and got as much of the water out of her hair as she could. She dressed in the jeans and pullover top she had brought, and combed her hair away from her face, letting it hang freely down her back.

Joe was waiting for her when she emerged. He had changed into a dark-blue pair of slacks and a light-blue shirt that appeared to have been left over from his evenings in Dallas restaurants and clubs, and his hair and face had fared better than hers had in the sun. Lynne cringed inwardly when she compared her appearance to his, but Joe didn't seem to notice the disparity. "Ready to go?" he asked. "I called over and we have a reservation for six forty-five."

"As ready as I'll ever be," Lynne said. She followed Joe out to the truck. They took the causeway across the bay to South Padre Island, the swanky resort strip that he said reminded him of a small Miami Beach. Joe drove until he spotted the fashionable new hotel where the restaurant was located.

He pulled in and parked in between a Cadillac and a Mercedes, and laughed out loud as he got out of the truck. "Doesn't quite fit, does it?" he asked, eyeing the beat-up old truck between the elegant new cars.

"I know the feeling," Lynne muttered under her breath. A couple of beautifully dressed women had come out of the hotel and were getting into the Cadillac.

"With that new car of yours?" Joe asked. "That little number would fit in anywhere."

Lynne started to explain, but Joe grabbed her by the hand and hurried her toward the door of the hotel. "I'm hungry," he said as they peered around the crowded lobby of the elegant hotel. Lynne felt a little more comfortable than she had at first, because half the people in the lobby were dressed in shorts or beach wraps, and most of their faces were sunburned. "Where do you suppose the restaurant is?" Joe asked.

Lynne pointed to a sign by the elevator. "On the top floor, the sign says."

"To the top floor it is, then," Joe said.

Lynne swallowed as she looked around at the sophisticated restaurant and its fashionable clientele. "Does this place have a dress code?" she whispered.

"Don't worry so much. Our money's just as good as it would be if we were dressed up," Joe said. And Lynne had to admit that the waiter didn't bat an eyelash; he seated them and said he hoped they would enjoy their dinner.

Lynne opened her menu and scanned it. "Anything here you can eat?" she asked. Most of the dishes were smothered in sauces, and the dessert menu took up half a page.

Joe looked down the menu. "The broiled fish with vegetables, a spinach salad, and the cheese-and-fruit plate for dessert. No problem. I've worked around the diet for so long, it's second nature to me now."

"Is is going to torture you if I get the chicken in a cream sauce?" Lynne asked.

Joe pretended to clutch his heart. "Oh, how could you do that to me? Make me sit here and watch you eat that? No, of course it won't bother me. I'll even buy you the biggest dessert on the menu."

They placed their order with the waiter, who immediately brought them a generous basket of bread. Lynne took some, and Joe tore a piece in half and nibbled that while Lynne consumed three pieces. They admired the magnificent view of the ocean, and Lynne had just about gotten over feeling uncomfortable about the way she looked when a gorgeous blonde in a red jump-suit sidled up the table and put her arm around Joe. "How have you been, stranger?" she asked him in a sultry voice. "Long time no see."

"Why, Grace, how are you?" Joe turned around in his chair and gave the beautiful woman a huge hug. Not content with just a hug, Grace presented her lips to his and Joe covered them in a quick, firm kiss. "It has been a while, hasn't it?"

"Too long, Gracie," Joe said, flashing her a smile. Lynne stared at the beautiful woman, and what little self-confidence she did have melted like an ice cream in the hot summer sun. Grace was small and quite shapely, and Lynne could tell that her striking shade of blond didn't come out of a bottle. She had the classical features of a photographic model, and her makeup served strictly to highlight and accent her features, not in any way to change them. Beside Grace, Lynne looked positively ratty, and she knew it. But it wasn't just her clothes. Lynne acknowledged to herself that, even if she had on Grace's chic jumpsuit and shoes, she would never look like Grace, not in a million years. Lynne felt a black cloud of depression descend on her. What she would give to look like that, just for one evening!

Grace let one hand linger in the hair at Joe's nape. "So where have you been lately, Joe, honey? I've missed you at the bar scene."

"Oh, Grace, didn't you know? I've moved down here permanently. You are now looking at a bona-fide cattle rancher." Lynne cleared her throat and Joe looked across the table and saw the dismay on her face. "Oh, I've been rude, haven't I?" he asked. "Lynne, this is Grace Loman from Dallas. Grace, this is Lynne Kosler. Lynne and I have been fishing today."

Grace extended her hand to Lynne. "I'm glad to meet you," she said, smiling sincerely, although she seemed a little taken aback by Lynne. Lynne wasn't sure if it was the clothes she was in or her unassuming features that had surprised the woman.

"I'm glad to meet you too," Lynne said, hoping the little green monster inside her wasn't showing too badly. "You're from Dallas, I gather?"

Grace nodded. "Joe and I were part of the same gang a few years back." She turned back to Joe. "Did you know that Duffy and Suzanne got married last month?" She rubbed the back of his neck with long red fingernails. "Isn't that a scream? Goody Two Shoes and the dirty old lady!"

Joe joined her in laughter. "You never can tell about people," he said.

Gracie lowered her voice. "So when can I come and see you and your beautiful ranch?" she asked. Her voice sank to a seductive purr. "I'd love to christen the barn with you."

Joe smiled his gorgeous smile and winked at Grace. "The barn and I can hardly wait," he teased. "It will be a welcome change from mares in foal."

And from homely INS agents delivering calves for him. Lynne's spirits plummeted even further. Joe was enjoying flirting with Grace. Lynne watched with blank eyes as Joe and Grace exchanged a few more provocative remarks, and after another kiss Grace disentangled herself from around Joe's neck and promised to tell all their old friends hello from him. Lynne watched Grace walk away from the table, depression and envy warring within her.

Joe settled back and sampled his salad. "Delicious," he said. "How's yours?"

Lynne shrugged. "Fine." She ate a couple more bites. In reality she could hardly taste the salad. The day's pleasure had been spoiled for her. Joe was obviously used to dating women like Grace, women who put her in the shade and always would. She must have misinterpreted the desire she had thought she saw in his eyes. She was just a fishing buddy to him, that was all.

Joe looked at Lynne's crestfallen face. "Look, I'm sorry if you feel that Gracie intruded on our evening. It's just that she's an old friend and I hated to put her off."

"Did you used to—uh, date her?" Lynne asked quietly. She almost slipped and asked if Joe had slept with her.

Joe shrugged. "A few times. She was no big deal, if that's what you're wondering."

"I couldn't help but wonder," Lynne admitted. She returned her attention to her salad. If Grace was no big deal, what kind of woman would be a big deal to Joe? Not a sunburned fishing buddy, that was for sure! She had been foolish to daydream that there might ever be anything between her and Joe. If Grace was anything to go by, Lynne wasn't his usual type at all.

The waiter brought their dinner and Lynne waded through hers dutifully, her pleasure in the day completely gone. Although she held up her end of the conversation, the wit and sparkle that had colored her earlier that day had disappeared. Weighted down by her own feelings of inadequacy and completely forgetting the passionate kiss she and Joe had shared the other night, she convinced herself that Joe saw her only as a friend. He would save his sensuality and his passion for a woman like Grace.

At first Joe was puzzled by the change in Lynne. What had he done to make her change like that? Was it him, or was Lynne jealous of Grace? Joe hadn't pegged Lynne as the sensitive type, but maybe she was. Apparently she had taken the silly teasing about christening the barn seriously, and it must have hurt her feelings. Joe was surprised and just a little bit pleased. He hadn't realized that Lynne cared that much for him.

They finished their dinner and Joe urged Lynne to get a dessert, ordering the fruit and cheese plate for himself. Lynne ordered a huge baked Alaska that she didn't really want, and then couldn't finish half the rich-tasting concoction. He paid for the meal and they started back toward Brownsville. The sun had set in a blaze of glory while they were eating, and the purple dusk was fading into the black of night. The bright lights of South Padre Island and the more subdued lights of Port Isabel danced in the waves of the ocean, their reflections broken into a thousand dancing stars in the rolling black water. The view revived Lynne's spirits some, but she was still feeling quiet and subdued when Joe pulled up to her apartment building an hour later. They had not talked much on the way home, and Joe had finally tuned into the local country-and-western station.

Lynne turned to Joe in the darkness of the cab. "Thanks for taking me today," she said. "I had a great time."

"So did I," Joe said. He got out of the truck and held the door for Lynne. "You can pick up your cooler tomorrow night." He gathered up her knapsack and started around the retaining wall.

Without thinking, Lynne made her usual vault over the wall. Joe stared open mouthed at her. "Did I really just see you jump over a four-foot wall?"

"Why shouldn't I jump over it? It was in the way, wasn't it?" Lynne asked irritably, brushing a strand of limp hair out of her face.

"Sorry I asked," Joe said. He trotted around the retaining wall and carried the knapsack up the stairs. Following Lynne into her apartment, he put the knapsack down on the kitchen table and then flopped down on the living-room couch. "You've been quiet and unhappy for the last two hours," he said, grinning wickedly. "Can I make it better?"

"I have not been unhappy," Lynne said as she stood awkwardly in the middle of the room.

"Yes, you have." Joe shook his finger at her accusingly. "You took Grace's routine seriously, didn't you? Shame on you, thinking I would christen the barn with Grace! It would scare the horses to death! Do you really think I would hurt my horses that way?"

In spite of herself Lynne started to smile. "It would itch if you did it in the hay," she said.

"Now, how did you know that?" Joe asked, and laughed out loud while Lynne turned a brilliant shade of red. "Come here, Lynne," he said softly, and patted the couch beside him. She sat down and he took her hand in his. "Lynne, I'm sorry if I neglected you and hurt your feelings this evening when Grace came by. She and I go back all the way to college days, and she's a friend. But she's just a friend, Lynne. That's all. We go through that routine every time we see each other. We don't mean anything by it. Now, can I do what I've been dying to do all day?"

"What's that?" Lynne asked.

"This," Joe said. He put his arms around Lynne and pushed her down a little into the sofa, staring down into her startled eyes. "I've wanted to kiss you since I came to pick you up this morning," he said, and nibbled her lips lightly with his. "It was all I could do not to ravish you out there on that boat when you were in that adorable little bikini of yours," he added, his lips touching light, feathery kisses on the sides of her mouth and her cheeks.

"Oh, Joe," Lynne breathed as his lips covered hers. Her mouth opening, Lynne gave herself up to the passion and desire she found in Joe's arms. His kisses deepened and her senses reeled as her hands found and caressed the warmth of his shoulders and nape. Her fingers greedy for the feel of him, she let herself explore the hard warmth of his body, stroking lower until she could touch the smooth contours of his chest. Joe groaned, framing her face with his hands. "You're not shy about touching me, are you?" he asked as her hands stroked down his back.

"No, and don't be shy about touching me," Lynne said, blushing a little at her own boldness.

Joe's eyes smoldered with sensuality. "You don't realize how much that pleases me," he said as his gaze traveled down her body. His lips grazed her lips and cheeks as his hands slowly made their way down her body, caressing first the soft skin of her neck and arms before finding the tenderness of one small breast. He tormented the tender bud with the tip of his thumb before placing a wet kiss through the thin fabric of her top.

Lynne's fingers found the buttons of Joe's shirt and worked a couple of them loose. "I want to see who I'm touching," she said as she slowly and deliberately unbuttoned the rest of Joe's shirt. "Your chest is as soft as I thought it would be," she said as she planted a tender kiss, her tongue darting out for a sensual caress.

Shivers of pleasure tore through Joe. "I want to see you," he said, tugging the knit shirt up and over Lynne's head in one swift motion. He gazed at her small breasts through the lace of her bra before he found the closure in the back and released it. Almost reverently, his hand reached out and caressed the gentle swell of her small breasts. "You're perfect, just perfect," he breathed, bending his head and caressing one nipple with his tongue.

Lynne gasped as a shaft of pure pleasure tore through her. "Joe, that's, oh . . ." she said as his lips traveled to the other breast, which he also caressed into a hard bud in his mouth. He gazed at her for a moment before his lips joined with hers again, the soft hair on his chest caressing her bare breasts. Lynne locked her arms around his neck and held him tightly to her, drinking in the passion and affection Joe was sharing with her. They kissed and caressed for long moments, both of them savoring the intimacy they had not expected to be so wonderful.

Finally Joe pulled away from her and sat up. "Lynne, honey, if I hold you any more tonight, I'm not going to be able to stop, and I don't think either one of us is ready for that yet, do you?"

Lynne shook her head as she sat up and pulled her shirt over her head. "You're right, it's much too soon. I'm not made that way. Unfortunately," she added dryly.

"Neither am I," Joe admitted. "I know men are supposed to be, but I'm just not."

"I'm glad," Lynne said, stroking his face.

"Lynne, will you promise not to be jealous of Grace?"

83

Joe asked. "I don't want you jealous of a woman I'm just friends with."

"I promise," Lynne said.

"Now, what time can you be out at the house tomorrow to eat your fish?" Joe asked, relieved that Lynne understood about Grace. It never occurred to him that her feelings might involve more than simple jealousy.

"Unless I call you or have somebody call you from the office, I can be there by six-thirty," Lynne said. "If I'm not, you go ahead and eat, and I'll eat what's left when I get there."

Joe kissed her gently. "You're a lovely and gracious woman to volunteer to eat the crumbs," he said. "Just kidding—I'll leave you plenty," he added when Lynne picked up a throw pillow to hit him with. "Thanks for the day." He rose from the couch. "I enjoyed it so much. Are you free next weekend?"

"Sunday," Lynne said.

"Want to spend the day riding?" Joe asked. "And I'll take you to a movie that night."

"Sounds great," Lynne said. She followed Joe out the door and stood on the porch until his truck was out of sight. Sighing, she sat down on the top step and stared across the street at a pair of teenagers necking in a parked car.

Joe had not understood her feelings tonight. She had been a little jealous of his flirting with Grace, but mostly she had envied Grace her beauty. Grace had matched Joe in looks, while she, Lynne, looked odd walking beside him. She wondered briefly how long Joe had actually dated Grace, but realized that it didn't really matter, not if he said Grace was no big deal. And he had made not one more date with her before he left, but two.

She and Joe had something between them, that Lynne was sure of. He couldn't have kissed her and caressed her as he had if it weren't something special. But she was up against a world full of beautiful women, and Joe wasn't blind—he could tell she was no beauty. Joe was interested in her now, but how long would it be before he wanted someone prettier to look at?

CHAPTER FIVE

Lynne climbed out of the cockpit of the old World War II bomber and wiped the sweat off her forehead. "It's like an oven in there," she said as she walked down the metal stairs positioned by the old airplane. "What on earth possessed us to come over here this afternoon? It's broiling out here!"

"It wasn't my idea," Joe said smugly, following her down the stairs. "As I recall, you wanted me to see all these neat old airplanes." He reached out and tugged Lynne's braid. "Not your smartest suggestion on record." Lynne had wanted Joe to see the fabulous collection of World War II combat aircraft housed at the Confederate Air Force Flying Museum in Harlingen, since he had never been there before.

"All right, I admit that it was my idea and that it's too hot. Sorry about that," Lynne said, fanning her face. A blistering July wind blew across the runway, stirring up the dust.

Joe stood up on his tiptoes and planted a quick kiss on her lips. "That's all right, you're forgiven." He sampled her lips once more. "I wish we weren't in a public place," he said. "I'd love to do this right."

"Hey, lady, why don't you find one your own size?" a cheeky voice called from a few feet away.

Lynne and Joe jumped apart and looked down at a boy of about ten or so. Lynne stared down her nose at the boy. "Kid, if you haven't tried it, don't knock it," she said. The little boy giggled and scampered off.

Joe took Lynne's hand and together they wandered into the next hangar, where the airplanes were all outrageously painted and decorated, much like custom vans. "Did that kid embarrass you?" Joe asked. Although Lynne's height no longer intimidated him, he still wished he were at least as tall as she was.

Lynne shook her head. "I can't help being tall," she said. In the two months that she and Joe had been going together, she had ceased to be sensitive about the height difference between them, although she still felt insecure about the rest of her appearance. "Besides, who else can reach the top shelves of your cabinets?" she teased.

"Just checking," Joe said. They looked around at the airplanes for a few more minutes, until the hangar became unbearable, and escaped to Joe's car, where they aimed the air-conditioner vents on their faces. "So where would you like to eat dinner?" Joe asked. "Is there anywhere here in Harlingen you particularly like?"

"Not really. Besides, it's early yet. Why don't we go back to your place and raid your deep freeze? Those steaks from the calf you butchered last month were delicious. If you'll stop by the apartment, I have a sack of fresh green beans and some Port wine cheese that would be delicious with it."

Joe took Lynne's hand in his and squeezed it. "I know what you're doing and I appreciate it," he said. The ranch had incurred several unexpected expenses in the last two months, and Joe was short on money at the moment. Lynne had suggested eating at his place or hers for the last three weeks.

"I would offer to take you out, but I'm short too," she admitted. "I splurged and bought a new saddle on Thursday."

"High time," Joe said. "That monstrosity you were using was an insult to Betsy!"

Lynne stuck her tongue out at Joe. She teased him about the beat-up old hat he was never without, and they laughed and joked with each other for a while. As the traffic started to thicken, Joe concentrated on his driving and Lynne stared out the window at the rolling green pasture. Every so often she glanced over at Joe, a pair of aviator sunglasses perched on his perfect nose and his forehead wrinkled in a frown of concentration, and she was tempted to reach out and touch him, to see if he was real and not just a beautiful dream. Lynne couldn't believe that she had managed to hold Joe's interest for so long a time. They had shared lots of good times together, fishing some weekends and riding others, shopping across the border in Matamoros. One notable evening, they barhopped on both sides of the border and Lynne sang "Ninety-nine Bottles of Beer" to Joe all the way home. They had also spent many evenings holding hands in Joe's porch swing, watching the stars come out, and to Lynne those had been the best times of all.

Lynne ran her finger down her nose. Joe had never said anything about her looks, or her lack of them. Her lack of beauty had never seemed to bother him, and it did not seem to have discouraged him from wanting to hold her and touch her. They had not become lovers yet, although they had shared many passionate kisses and caresses.

Lynne knew that if Joe didn't tire of her before too much longer, they would be sharing that ultimate intimacy. On one level Lynne welcomed the thought of making Joe her lover, of sharing herself with him in that way, but on another level she was worried. There had been women in Joe's past, beautiful women, and Lynne wondered how she would compare to them. It wasn't that Lynne was all that modest with him anymore—he had seen her in a bikini on a number of occasions now, but she still felt very insecure. She hoped Joe wouldn't be disappointed in her if and when the time came.

They had stopped by Lynne's apartment and picked up the vegetables and cheese, and Lynne cooked the beans while Joe grilled a couple of steaks in his backyard on an ancient charcoal grill. Joe had painted the kitchen two weeks ago, and now the formerly drab room fairly sparkled with homey cheer, so Lynne set the table in there and made a fruit salad for Joe and baked a potato for herself. They lingered over supper, enjoying each other's company. After doing the dishes, Joe wanted to check on one of the cows in the pen, so Lynne made herself another glass of iced tea and sat down in the porch swing. She pushed the swing back and forth with one foot, sipping her tea and enjoying the warm summer breeze on her face.

Joe stood for a minute at the door of the barn and gazed at Lynne, her movements languid as she sipped her drink and watched the sun go down. She was quite a woman, and Joe considered himself lucky to know her. He desired her in a way in which he had never desired any other woman in his life. Before, he had wanted a woman for her body, her physical attributes, and only later had he cared about her as a person, if he ever did.

But with Lynne, he had cared for her as a person from the beginning, and his physical desire had been secondary. Secondary, but very, very strong. Joe felt the tightening in his midsection that he always experienced when he thought about Lynne, and wondered what she would say if he asked her to spend the night.

But Joe had another favor he wanted to ask of her. It was a huge one; he hoped she would get him out of a bind. He crossed the yard and sat down beside her in the swing. "Everything's fine out there," Joe said. "She doesn't look any sicker."

"That's good," Lynne said.

"Lynne, I have a big favor to ask of you," Joe said suddenly.

"As long as you don't want me to get you any illegal help, ask away," Lynne teased.

"Not illegal, but I could sure use some help," Joe admitted. "Les Kovaks, my roommate from college, is turning thirty next Saturday. In an impulsive moment last month I invited a few of our friends to come down for a party, and they invited a few friends they were sure I'd love to see, and so on. Now I have between thirty and forty people descending on me next Saturday afternoon, and I don't know the first thing about throwing a party! Can you help me, Lynne?"

Lynne was quiet for a moment. "Is anybody going to christen the barn?"

"With this crowd you never can tell," he quipped. He and Lynne laughed together.

"Sure, I'll put together something for you and your friends," Lynne said. "How elegant? Indoors or out? Mexican or Western theme? Just tell me what you want and how much you want to spend and I can do it."

"Oh, nothing fancy. How about a Mexican theme and cheap?"

"All right, how about a *fajita* party?" Lynne asked. "All you have to do is grill the *fajitas* and make the guacamole and *pico de gallo*. Your guests do the rest. And it's about as inexpensive as you can get."

"Sounds great." He put his arm around Lynne and pulled her close to him. "Thank you, Lynne," he said, and his lips covered hers.

Lynne gave herself over to the tender, sensual intimacy of his embrace. She opened her mouth to his, touching and tasting, feeling her breasts swell against Joe's chest. Side by side on the swing, they were pressed together from waist to knee, their thighs close together, their hips touching. Joe groaned with pleasure as Lynne stroked the muscles of his neck and shoulders. "We can't go on like this much longer," he murmured as he found and caressed her breast through the fabric of her blouse. "I want you too badly."

"I want you, too, Joe," Lynne whispered.

Joe stared into her eyes. "Tonight?"

Lynne shook her head. "I'm not protected," she admitted. "And I have to get up at four for an early shift. I want us to have plenty of time to be together. And I don't want to have to get dressed and go home."

Joe kissed her lips tenderly. "You have a point," he said. "But I don't want to wait forever."

"It won't be forever," Lynne promised, although her feelings of inadequacy were suddenly worse than ever, and she was glad that she had a way out tonight. She was terribly afraid that Joe would find her lacking as a lover.

Lynne promised Joe she would start on the party tomorrow, and shared a few more lingering kisses with him

91

before he drove her home. Even though she had to be up at four, she sat down at the kitchen table and made a list of the things she would need for the get-together. Joe didn't know it, but she could give a bang-up good party, and she was going to give his friends from Dallas the best time they'd ever had!

Lynne worked on the party all week. Without telling Joe, she expanded the menu a little, adding rice and *chalupas,* and buñuelos for dessert. Since the house was so dismal inside, she decided to disguise the drab interior with colorful decorations, and spent most of Wednesday, her day off, in the Matamoros market buying paper flowers, piñatas, and a couple of the inexpensive, colorful tablecloths for the inside tables. Although Joe's friends were bringing liquor, she and Joe bought a couple of bottles of tequila, and Lynne spent Thursday evening in the grocery store, purchasing the rest of what she needed for the party. She picked out fabric for a new dress and took it to the dressmaker, and she went back to Maria's on Friday after work for a final fitting. While Maria made the final alterations on the dress, Lynne picked up the bunuelos and tortillas she had ordered from her favorite bakery. A thought occurred to her and she dialed Joe's number.

Joe answered the phone sounding harried. "What is it, hon? The bull just knocked down a section of fence and got out. I have to catch him before he gets too far away."

"I was going to ask if you'd had time to clean your house," Lynne said. "But I'll reconsider."

"Oops, I forgot. I'll clean it a little when I get the bull in. See you."

Lynne groaned—she had seen Joe's "clean it a little." She ate a quick sandwich and gathered up her sweeper and a sack of various cleansers. She found Joe's house deserted, and had vacuumed and mopped the entire house by the time a sour-faced Joe drove up with his belligerent bull in the trailer behind the pickup. "Oh, Lynne, you didn't have to clean the house too! You've done so much already. Besides, they'll only be in the living room and kitchen."

"That's what you think," Lynne said. "They'll be all over this house, Joe! They're going to be dying of curiosity."

"Let me go unload that bull and I'll help you," Joe said. He returned a few minutes later and the two of them made quick work of the rest of the house. Lynne left Joe's around nine and crawled into bed an hour later, exhausted. Joe owed her one for this!

Lynne slept late the next morning. She dressed in an old pair of shorts and packed all of her cosmetics and her new underwear in a flight bag, and within an hour she was driving through Joe's front gate. She waved to Joe in the pasture as she drove by, and hung her new dress in his closet. She would do all the cooking and decorating before she dressed for the party. It only took her an hour or so to decorate the living and dining rooms and set up a buffet, but preparing the food took a little longer. Still, Lynne had allowed herself plenty of time to finish preparing the food and get ready for the party before the first guests arrived at four. No more of Joe's friends were going to see her looking the way Grace had seen her!

Lynne was finished even earlier than she had anticipated, since Joe came in around noon and pitched in with peeling and chopping the *pico de gallo,* both of them valiantly fighting the onion fumes and wiping the tears out of their eyes. Since she wanted to keep the front bathroom clean, Lynne insisted they both use the back one, and Joe volunteered to let Lynne have the bathroom first. After showering, she put on her underwear, but she couldn't find Joe's hair drier. She stuck her head out the bathroom door. "Joe!" she called.

"What?" Joe cried as he came up off his bed.

"Sorry, I didn't realize you were right here," Lynne said softly. "Do you have a hair drier I could use?"

"It's in the cabinet over the toilet," Joe said.

Lynne found the hair drier and plugged it in, not realizing that the bathroom door had stayed open a little behind her. Joe watched through the door as Lynne picked up her long, straight hair and dried it section by section, leaving it to fall down past her shoulders. Her movements were unconsciously sensual, the lace of her bra revealing just a hint of the pink of her nipples. As Joe watched her, he wished Lynne could share his bathroom with him all the time—it seemed so right for her to be in there, sharing his soap and his washcloths and using his hair drier.

Lynne poked her head out the door a second time. "Can you hand me my dress?" she asked. If she noticed that Joe had been watching her, she gave no indication.

Joe handed Lynne her dress. A moment later she emerged from the bathroom in the new party dress Maria had made. It was a bright rose cotton, and it accented what curves Lynne did have. Joe let out a long, low whistle. "You're gonna knock 'em dead, sweetheart."

Lynne blushed with pleasure. "I'm glad you think so," she said. She sat down at the dresser and got out her makeup.

Instead of going to the shower, Joe sat down at the foot of the bed. "Mind if I watch?" he asked. "I love it when a woman puts on her makeup. It's such a feminine thing to do."

"No, I don't mind," Lynne murmured distractedly, her mind on how to best make her face for the party. As Joe watched her, he was once again seized by the feeling that Lynne belonged here in this house and this bedroom with him. He wanted her to sit at the dresser and do her face every day while he watched. And at night he wanted her to step from the shower, dripping wet and naked, and fall together with him into a passionate embrace.

"Joe," Lynne said softly. "Joe?"

"Huh? What?" Joe blinked his eyes and stared at Lynne.

"Must have been some daydream," she said softly.

"A beautiful one," he agreed. "What did you want?"

"The only shoes I could find that looked right had a heel on them," Lynne said. "I'm sorry."

"Don't be," Joe assured her, but he decided to wear his new cowboy boots with a two-inch heel, instead of the old, comfortable loafers he loved to wear.

The first car pulled up just as Joe was combing his hair into place and Lynne put the finishing touches on the dining room table. Joe slid into his new boots and hurried to the front door. Lynne joined him as a good-looking man and a gorgeous redheaded woman got out of a BMW and walked up to the house. "Les, Sharon, how are you?" Joe asked, and engulfed first the woman and then the man in big hugs.

"Joe, you son of a gun, we miss you!" Les said as he and Joe shook hands.

"Yes, when are you giving this up and coming back to Dallas?" Sharon asked.

"Are you kidding? Never!" Joe said. "I love it out

here." He turned around and put his arm around Lynne. "Les, Sharon, I'd like you to meet Lynne Kosler. Lynne, Les and Sharon Kovaks."

"How do you do," Lynne murmured, extending her hand.

Sharon's gaze flickered upward to Lynne's face as she took Lynne's extended hand. "I'm glad to meet you," she said. "Are you a cousin of Joe's?"

"No, Lynne and I are dating," Joe said. "She put this party together for me."

Sharon couldn't disguise her surprise, although she tried to. "Oh. Did you meet in town?"

"No, I met her when she came out here to round up all my wetbacks." Joe laughed. "She's with INS."

Les extended his hand to Lynne. "Well, how many did he have?" he asked teasingly.

"Uh, two, but they were just along for the ride," Lynne stammered. Sharon's obvious surprise when she learned that Joe and Lynne were dating had shaken Lynne a little.

"Come on, I'll show you around before I start the charcoal," Joe said, taking Sharon by the arm.

Lynne looked out the window and saw another car coming up the drive, but Joe and his guests had disappeared. A couple of good-looking young executive types got out and came up to the house. "Is this the Stockton ranch?" one of them asked.

"Yes, it is," Lynne said. "I'm Lynne Kosler. Joe's out back with Les and Sharon."

"Hi, I'm Mel Turner, and this is Randy Williams," the older of the two men said. "It's Lynne, right? Glad to meet you, Lynne. Have you known Joe long?"

"We've only been dating a couple of months," Lynne

said. Again, Joe's friends looked surprised that he was dating her. Lynne smiled at them, hoping her hurt did not show. "Would you care for a drink?"

"I'll take some iced tea, if you have it," Randy said. "It was a long, hot drive down here."

They followed Lynne out to the kitchen. "Are you staying with Joe tonight?" she asked.

"No, we're driving as far back as Corpus tonight after the party and spending a couple of days there with relatives," Mel said.

Lynne poured them both a glass of iced tea. "Whenever you're ready for anything stronger, let me know. We have a keg on ice out in the back."

"Will do," the men said, and they wandered out the back door. Lynne started to offer her services as a guide, but heard another knock at the front door and went to answer it.

Lynne and Joe greeted a steady stream of new arrivals for the next hour. Lynne would just be getting tea poured or drinks mixed for one group when another carload would come up the drive. Lynne felt her spirits sinking by the minute as Joe introduced her to his friends. They were surprised, every one of them, that Joe was dating her. One woman even teased Joe about Lynne's not exactly being his usual type, bringing a flush of embarrassment to his cheeks. Had every one of his girlfriends in the past been raving beauties or something?

Joe started the grill about five. Lynne, who was tired of being introduced to Joe's friends, escaped gratefully to the kitchen, where she warmed the tortillas and the rice. She was just mixing herself a Scotch and soda when Sharon Kovaks came in the back door, waving her glass in front of her. "Lynne, help, do you have some plain cold water? It's sweltering out there!"

Lynne took Sharon's glass and fixed her some ice water. "Want me to put something in this?" she asked.

Sharon made a face. "I'd love to, but my OB says no until after the baby's born. I can't smoke either. I can hardly wait to go back to my vices!"

"Oh, you're having a baby?" Lynne asked. She loved babies and hoped to have children of her own someday.

"Yes, finally. It took us two years on the thermometer before we connected. Les thought he had a dud there for a while." She took the water glass from Lynne. "Well, thanks." Sharon took her water and darted out the door.

Lynne shrugged and turned back to the beans. She would have enjoyed talking to Sharon some more, but she guessed the woman wanted to return to her friends.

Lynne set everything out in the dining room, buffet style, so that when Joe had the first of the meat done at six all she had to do was slice it into thin *fajita* strips. Joe's friends served themselves and sat around the living room and front porch to eat their meal. Lynne sat down in the living room with some of them, letting the gossip and the chatter float around her ears. She had nothing in common with these trendy, upwardly mobile city people, and could contribute very little to their conversation. A few questions were directed her way, but for the most part Joe's friends ignored her.

Joe cooked the last of the meat about seven. Most of the others had eaten, and he and Lynne made themselves thick tacos and sat down on the couch. "You did a bang-up good job, Lynne," he said. "I haven't had this much fun at a party in a long time."

"I'm glad you're enjoying it," Lynne said. Even if she

wasn't having the time of her life, she was glad Joe was enjoying himself. She maneuvered her taco into her mouth for another bite.

"And isn't the gang just great?" Joe asked.

"Great," Lynne said, hoping Joe didn't hear the irony she felt. She had found his friends very uncomfortable to be around.

"Yeah, I have no desire to go back to Dallas, but I do miss them," Joe admitted.

"Hey, Joe, do you still have your stereo?" Randy Williams asked, banging on the front door. "That concrete slab out behind the house would make a great dance floor."

"Yes, it would, wouldn't it? May as well use it for something. I won't have the money to make it into another room for years." Joe's uncle had started at one time to add to the house, but never got any farther than a foundation. "The stereo's in my bedroom. I'll help you hook it up."

Joe downed his tacos quickly and left Lynne alone on the couch. She nibbled her taco, her appetite gone. Ignoring the sounds coming from outside, she cleaned up some of the mess in the living room, and was about to start on the kitchen when Joe stuck his head through the door. "Come on, Lynne, the dancing's about to start. We can clean up later."

Shrugging, Lynne followed Joe out the back door and around to the side of the house. Randy and a couple of the other guys had set up Joe's stereo and selected a disco recording by the Bee Gees. Before long Joe's friends were gyrating in the middle of the concrete dance floor. Lynne, who could hold her own while dancing, admired Joe's slick moves and figured he had spent a lot of time in Dallas discos.

Randy played several fast dances in a row before someone in the crowd called for a slow number. Lynne started to duck out of this one, but Joe took her into his arms and pulled her close to him. Lynne could feel Joe's warm breath on her neck as he started to move with the slow, haunting song about a lost love. She snuggled closer to Joe and was about to lose herself in the pleasure of dancing with him when she heard a snicker from behind her.

Joe felt her stiffen in his arms. "Relax," he said when she tried to pull away from him. Lynne opened her eyes and was surprised to find Joe's face beet red. "We'd look a whole lot sillier if I didn't have on these damned high-heeled boots!"

Lynne nodded and relaxed in his arms. "You're right," she whispered, bending her head to his ear. "It's their problem, not ours." But she noticed that Joe did not hold her quite so close for the rest of the dance.

The next dance was fast, and she excused herself, pleading thirst and promising Joe she would bring him a club soda from the kitchen. Lynne mixed herself a drink and poured Joe his club soda, and was about to go out when she heard two voices, one of them Sharon's, outside the back door. "I mean, Janice, can you believe Joe moving out here in the sticks? And the damned funny thing is, he really seems to like it! I'd be going crazy about now."

"Maybe he already is." Janice snickered. "Either that or he's gone blind. Did you get a load of that woman he's dating down here? You could have knocked me over with a feather when he said he was going with her. Really, have you ever seen a face like hers?"

"Yeah, on my daddy's horse," Sharon said. "And weren't they a hoot dancing together? I know, she isn't Joe's usual type, that's for sure."

"I wonder what he sees in her," Janice said. "He's always gone for pretty little blondes. Remember Suzy Thomas? Now, there was Joe's type!"

Lynne backed away from the door as Janice launched into a detailed description of Joe's old girlfriend, not wanting to hear a catalogue of the other girl's virtues. Blinking back tears, she circled through the house and went out the front door, glad the dark of the night could hide the red in her cheeks and the moisture in her eyes. Sharon and Janice were cruel, just plain cruel. She bet every person here was thinking the same thing Sharon and Janice were thinking, even if they weren't saying it out loud.

Lynne considered getting into her car and going home, but she had too much pride to let these people run her off like that. So she stuck out three more hours of the party, spending most of her time in the shadows around the dance floor except when Joe dragged her out for a dance. Joe's friends could mix their own drinks in the kitchen. She had played hostess all she intended to.

Joe put his arm around Lynne and sighed with relief as the last car disappeared down the dirt road at eleven-thirty. It was much earlier than their parties usually broke up in Dallas, but most of his friends had made hotel reservations on South Padre Island for the weekend, and would be continuing the party over there. Joe had more or less promised to join them, but he had a lot to do tomorrow, even if it was Sunday. Still, he had missed his friends and had enjoyed seeing them. "Nice party," Joe said to Lynne as they walked back to the house. "You did a wonderful job."

"Thank you," Lynne replied. Most of Joe's friends had told her the same thing, at least to her face. She stuck out her tongue at the mess in the living room and got a plastic garbage sack out of the kitchen. "I'll help you get some of this cleaned up, but then I have to go. I have to go in for a few hours early tomorrow morning."

Joe picked up a stack of dirty paper plates and shoved them into the sack. "Say, did you ever talk to Marta and Jeff Martin? I had hoped you three would get acquainted."

"Only when you introduced us," Lynne said, putting a stack of dirty paper cups into the sack.

"You should have talked to Marta," Joe admonished her. "She's an accomplished artist. You would have enjoyed her very much."

"Was she the one in the red jeans and the black top?"

"Yes, she was," Joe said.

"I sat next to her for thirty minutes during dinner. She didn't say a word to me," Lynne said bitterly.

Joe was surprised and it showed. "That isn't like Marta," he said. "She usually talks your ear off."

"Well, she didn't this time." Lynne carried the leftover *pico de gallo* into the kitchen.

Joe followed her with the bowl of darkening guacamole. "How about Amy Kendall? She's a stockbroker now."

"No, I didn't even talk to her either," Lynne said. She went back into the dining room and started stacking the *fajita* platters.

Joe was waiting for her when she returned to the kitchen. "Well, then, just who did you talk to?" he asked.

He had been hoping all week that Lynne would like his friends.

"I talked to Sharon Kovaks for exactly two and a half minutes," Lynne said. "I talked to Randy Williams a little, and some guy who's into real estate. And that's about it."

"For heaven's sake, Lynne, why didn't you visit a little more? I didn't mean for you to be the maid today."

"I would have, Joe, if your friends had wanted to talk to me. But they ignored me completely for the entire evening." Sharon and Janice's cruel words popped back into her mind. "I'm sorry, Joe, but your friends aren't the nicest bunch of people in the world."

"How can you say a thing like that?" Joe demanded. "What do you know about my friends?"

"Enough," Lynne said acidly as she jerked the dirty tablecloth off the table. "I don't like them, Joe. They're rude and they're shallow."

Joe thought of all the things he and Les had done together, and of the times Les and the others had lent him a helping hand. "My friends are not rude and shallow, Lynne," he said angrily. "They're some of the nicest, sweetest people on the face of this earth. And you would have found that out, if you'd bothered to talk to any of them. I resent the hell out of your attitude toward them."

"They didn't want to talk to me, Joe," Lynne said bitterly, fighting back tears. "They wanted to talk, all right, but they wanted to talk about me, not to me. And you're welcome to resent my attitude toward them. I happen to resent the hell out of their attitude toward me." She threw the dirty tablecloth at Joe and stalked into his bedroom, grabbing up her makeup case but leaving her dirty clothes behind. Tears were streaming down her face when she returned to the living room. "All I can say is, if that's the sweetest bunch of people on the face of this earth, I feel sorry for the rest of the world." She slammed the door behind her and cried most of the way home, cursing Joe and his friends every other breath. How could he defend cruel people like that?

What on earth had brought that on? Lynne was usually the soul of fairness, but tonight she had condemned his friends without even giving them a chance. That wasn't like Lynne. Not after she had knocked herself out to give them a fantastic party. And that hadn't been just anger in her eyes. Lynne had been hurt this evening. Something had been said or done that had hurt her terribly.

Absently, Joe carried the tablecloth out to the washer and shoved it in. Something had to have happened to set Lynne off like that. But what? What had happened to make her feel as she did? Joe started to look for his wallet and car keys, but checked his watch first and groaned. It was after midnight and they both had to work tomorrow. It was too late to go see Lynne tonight, but tomorrow he would the minute she got home from work, and find out what had upset her so.

Joe, running the razor over his face, glowered at his tired-looking reflection in the mirror. He hadn't slept too well, worrying about Lynne most of the night, and he dreaded finding out whatever had happened last night to upset her so. He had to admit that some of the women could be a little catty on occasion, and wondered if one of them had made a disparaging crack about the decorations or the food. Maybe that was it. Anyway, he would get to the bottom of it.

Joe finished shaving and reached into the drawer where he kept his insulin. As he did every morning, he swabbed his forearm with alcohol and injected a dose of insulin with a disposable syringe, tossing the syringe into the trash can. He dressed and made breakfast, and was just starting his meal when he heard loud pounding on the front door.

Joe swallowed his orange juice and ran to the front, hoping his unexpected guest might be Lynne. He opened the door and found his neighbor from down the road, Hannah Michaels, with a worried expression on her face. "Mr. Stockton, I thought I'd better come and tell you. That bull of yours must have torn the fence down again. Half your herd's out on the highway."

Joe's face turned white. "Oh, God, no." Not only could his animals get lost or killed, he as their owner would be personally liable for the car and any injury to the occupants if a car hit one of them. He couldn't afford that! "Mrs. Michaels, thank you," Joe said, and he grabbed his hat off the dining room table. He would have to round up his workers, if they all weren't too hung over to get out of bed, and some of them would have to mend the fence while he and the others found the cattle and stayed with them until the fence was back up. He could cheerfully kill that devil of a red bull!

"Mr. Stockton, my husband said he would be glad to help you," Hannah volunteered.

"Thank you, Mrs. Michaels," Joe said. He grabbed the hard candy he was never without, dropping several of the pieces on the floor, and rushed out of his house toward the worker's cabins, forgetting Lynne, their fight, and everything else—including the breakfast no diabetic was ever supposed to go without.

CHAPTER SIX

Lynne walked in the door of her apartment and sank down on the couch, putting her head in her hands. Thank goodness Ben had let her off early today! She hadn't slept more than a couple of hours last night, and she and Larry Martínez had spent the early hours of the morning tracking a group of aliens who were known to be armed. Much to Lynne's relief the aliens surrendered without shooting at them, and Ben had seen her at the detention center and told her to go on home. Her eyes were no longer swollen, but they were still bloodshot from all the crying she had done last night. How could Joe have defended his friends the way he had? After what those two women had said about her?

Lynne jumped when the telephone rang. She hesitated to answer, thinking it might be Joe, but she remembered that Laura had promised to call about riding this afternoon. "Hello," she said tiredly into the receiver.

"Whew, you sound beat," Laura said sympathetically. "Did the party do you in last night?"

"You might say that," Lynne admitted.

"Would you and Joe like to come and go riding with Tony and Laurina? They're going out in a little while."

"Joe won't be with me, but I'd love to come. I'll change and be right over."

"Is Joe working this morning?" Laura asked. "He's working too hard these days."

"I don't know what Joe's doing this morning, and I don't really care," Lynne said coolly.

"Oops," Laura said. "We'll see you in a little while."

Lynne hung up the telephone and changed into a pair of jeans and a knit shirt with spaghetti straps. She put a change of clothes in her duffel bag and drove out to Laura's. Silently Lynne cursed herself for having let on that anything was wrong between her and Joe. Laura and Tony had become fond of Joe in the last two months, and Laura would want to know what had happened between them. Yet, it might help to talk to Laura—not that Laura, with her fascinating sensuality, would have the vaguest idea how Lynne felt about herself.

Lynne drove up the gravel road that led to their sprawling new ranch house and parked in the driveway. She got her clean clothes out of the trunk, and was walking up the sidewalk when a tiny, dark-haired dynamo of a little girl ran out the front door and wrapped her arms around Lynne's legs. "Auntie Lynne, Auntie Lynne, I'm so glad to see you! Mommy said you were going to go riding with us, and that you would eat lunch with us."

"I'm glad to see you too, hon," Lynne said, and hugged the little girl. She straddled Laurina across one hip and carried her into the house, where Laura's husband Tony was waiting for her. "Are you ready to go, Auntie Lynne?" he teased, his lilting accent lifting Lynne's spirits just a little. "Laurina's been so impatient—haven't you, little one?"

"I'll have lunch waiting when you get back," Laura

said, poking her head around the corner. "We can talk then."

Lynne raised her eyebrow but said nothing. She and Tony saddled the horses, and they spent over an hour out in the pasture. Tony did most of the talking, wondering out loud what was going to happen to the local ranchers if the drought did not break. Lynne listened and occasionally asked him a question. It wouldn't hurt Tony so much, his family had money and the ranch was more of a tax write-off than anything else, but ranchers like Joe would be hard hit if the drought didn't break soon. Lynne wondered what Joe was doing this morning and if he had even given a thought to their argument. She thought he probably had, but she doubted if it had bothered him the way it had bothered her.

Tony and Lynne turned back about noon, and by the time they had unsaddled the horses, Laura had laid out a light lunch of cold cuts and fruit in the cool breakfast room. Lynne and Tony offered to change clothes, but Laura assured them that they were still socially acceptable, and the four of them sat down around Laura's table. "How did the party go?" Laura asked as she cut Laurina a piece of ham into small pieces.

"It went beautifully," Lynne admitted. "Joe's friends ate and drank and danced the evening away, and they all told me what a good job I'd done on the party."

Laura and Tony looked at each other. This wasn't what they had expected. "But you sounded angry with Joe this morning when I called you," Laura persisted.

"Would it do any good if I said I didn't want to talk about it?" Lynne asked dryly.

"Probably not," Tony admitted. "Laura's been worried ever since you talked to her this morning."

108

"And you haven't?" Laura asked.

"Yes, Lynne, I've been worried about you too," Tony said. "Your eyes are red like you've been crying. What happened? Did you and Joe have a fight?"

"Tony, we had one whale of a fight," Lynne admitted. "I walked out of his house angry, and I haven't seen him since."

"But what did you fight over," Laura asked, "if the party was a success like you said it was?"

"His friends." Lynne spat out the words. "They have to be the meanest bunch of people I've ever met." She bit into a slice of rolled-up ham. "But Joe can't see this. He thinks they're God's gift to mankind."

Tony and Laura saw the hurt in Lynne's eyes. "What did these people do to you to make you feel like that about them?" Laura asked.

"It's the way they looked at me!" Lynne said. "When they found out that Joe and I were dating, they looked like they couldn't believe it. Some of them came out and said it. Good grief, am I *that* ugly?"

"Oh, Lynne, you're not ugly!" Laura cried. "I'm sure that's not what they meant at all."

"Maybe they're used to seeing Joe with teachers, or nurses, or something," Tony added. "I'm sure it wasn't the way you look."

"Want to bet?" Lynne asked bitterly. "I heard a couple of the women talking about me. They were laughing about Joe's new horse-faced girlfriend, and were talking about one of his beautiful exes when I couldn't stand it anymore and got out of earshot."

"And Joe defended these women? The man should be shot!" Tony snapped. "I have a good mind to go over there right now and tell him what I think."

109

Laura laid a restraining hand on Tony's arm. "Just a minute, love, before you go storming out to Joe's ranch. Lynne, does Joe know what you overheard?"

Lynne shook her head miserably. "We blew up and I left. How could I tell him a thing like that?"

"I think you should, Lynne," Tony said. "He should know what kind of people he calls his friends."

"Yes, he needs to know," Laura agreed. "Otherwise, how is he to know why you don't like these people?"

"But I can't tell him!" Lynne protested. "I'm too ashamed."

"It's his friends who ought to be ashamed, not you," Tony said tartly.

"Lynne, you and that man have a good thing going," Laura said gently. "It would be a shame to let it go over something like this."

"I guess you're right," Lynne said.

"And, Lynne," Laura added hesitantly, "please don't be so sensitive about your looks. You're not ugly, you're far from it, and in the long run, looks don't matter that much, anyway. They really don't."

"Oh, don't they?" Lynne asked dryly, and Laura could tell that her suggestion had fallen on deaf ears.

"Now, I think you should finish your lunch and go on out to Joe's," Tony said. "Don't wait for him to come to you. Don't let it fester."

"All right," Lynne said. "I'll go on out to see him this afternoon."

"That's the way," Laura said. "Would you like some more ham and cheese?"

Joe wiped the sweat off his forehead and ate the last piece of hard candy he had with him. If he didn't get these idiot cattle rounded up and back in the pasture pretty quickly, he was going to be very sick very soon. But he couldn't quit what he was doing. His foreman had left the ranch early this morning, before the cattle had gotten out, and Joe and the other laborers still had to herd these in and round up the stragglers. The men would be lost if he wasn't there to supervise them. "Come on, you fat, lazy cow," he said irritably as he flicked his whip over the rump of number 223. "Get your big behind over there with the rest of the renegades."

In response the cow looked back at him and chewed on her cud. Slowly she ambled over to where the rest of the cattle were being kept in a loose herd by a couple of the hands. Joe fought the cold sweat he could feel engulfing him. "Is the fence fixed yet?" he asked one of the men.

"Yes, señor, it's almost done," one of the workers said.

"Then let's get this bunch down through the gate and I'll go back for the stragglers later," Joe said. He and the others guided the cattle down the road, making sure none wandered away from the herd. The cattle were cooperative enough, but they had gotten out nearly a mile from the gate and some had wandered even farther than that, and by the time they had reached the front gate Joe was trembling and his cold sweat was much worse. One of the workers asked him a question twice before he answered it. As the cows ambled through the gate, he thought he heard a car drive up, but it wasn't until Lynne had called his name twice that he turned around. "Huh?" he asked as he stared down at her.

Lynne stared up into Joe's sweating face. Something was wrong with him. She had called his name twice before he had answered her, and his expression was vague, detached somehow. "What's wrong, Joe?"

"Uh, the cows got out this morning," he said slowly. "I have to round them up."

"Is this all that got out?" Lynne asked.

"Uh, I don't think so," he said. He reached into his pocket. "Out of candy."

Lynne's mind raced as she tried to remember everything she knew about insulin shock. "When did you eat last?"

Joe thought a minute. "Part of breakfast," he said.

Lynne looked at her watch. It was nearly three, and Joe should have eaten since then. "What can I do to help you?" she asked. "Do you need to go to the hospital? Joe? Joe, do you need to go to the hospital?"

Joe shook his head. Lynne reached out and touched one of his hands. It was cold and clammy. "Get down off that horse before you fall off," she ordered him. "I'll get these cattle through the gate for you."

Joe dismounted and leaned against the Fiero while Lynne and the workers got the cattle in the pasture. She opened the door of the Fiero and pushed Joe in. "I'm taking you in to the doctor," she said.

"Huh? No, just take me to the gas station up the way and buy me a Coke," he said.

"Are you sure?" Lynne asked.

Joe nodded his head and Lynne sped down the highway to the nearest service station. She got Joe a Coke and watched him closely as he drank it. Within five minutes he had begun to perk up considerably, and within ten minutes the cold sweat had disappeared and Joe seemed to be all right. "Thanks," he said, and handed Lynne the bottle. "I didn't take enough candy with me this morning."

"What happened?" Lynne asked.

"The bull knocked down the fence last night and half the herd got loose. I've spent the day rounding them up. I still have a half dozen stragglers loose out there I have to go get."

"That's what you think," Lynne said, starting the Fiero. "You're going to eat something and then lie down for a little while. I'll gather up the wanderers."

"You don't have to—"

"Shut up and get well," Lynne said curtly, her fingers trembling with aftershock now that Joe was all right. "You scared me just now, you know."

"I'm sorry," Joe said helplessly.

Lynne leaned over and kissed his cheek. "No, I'm sorry," she said gently. "I was scared and I took it out on you. But will you please go eat and rest and let me get the rest of the cattle in? I'll cook you a proper supper when I'm finished."

Joe nodded. Lynne dropped him by the house and got on Joe's horse, which was tied by the front gate. It took her over an hour to round up the six or so stragglers and get them into the pasture, and she was worried about Joe. When she returned to the house, she found the remnants of a cheese-and-fruit snack he had made himself, and Joe asleep on the couch. Lynne sat down in the wing chair and stared into his face for a minute. He had deep circles under his eyes, and Lynne suspected that he had slept as little as she had last night. She kissed his forehead lightly and got her clean clothes out of the car. She showered and dressed in the shorts and top she had brought.

Joe's eyes flickered open as she was reentering the living room. "Did you get them all in?" he asked.

"Every blasted one of them," she said cheerfully. "Now, what would you like for supper?"

"You don't have to cook supper for me," Joe protested.

"Stop being the big, strong hero and let me help you," Lynne said. "Is there any fish left from that fishing trip last weekend?"

Joe nodded. Lynne thawed the fish under the hot water, seasoned it, and put it under the broiler. She made a big salad and opened a can of black-eyed peas. She wasn't sure if Joe could have tartar sauce, but she made enough for two anyway and set it on the table. "Feel better?" she asked as Joe sat down across from her.

"Much," Joe said. He took a bite of his fish. "You cook this better than that fancy restaurant on South Padre Island."

"Thank you." Lynne sampled a bite of the fish. "It is good, isn't it?"

"You look tired," Joe said. "I'm sorry you had to round up my cows for me, after working all day."

"I only worked for a few hours early this morning," Lynne said, "then I went riding with Tony and Laurina."

"I'm glad you came when you did," Joe admitted. "I don't know how much longer I could have lasted."

"Do you get sick like that often?" Lynne asked.

"Almost never," Joe replied. "As long as I stay on the diet and eat regularly, I'm fine. And I don't abuse it—I eat when and what I'm supposed to." He made a face. "Although sometimes I sure would love a bowl of ice cream."

"I'm sorry you can't eat what you want," Lynne said quietly.

"Please don't feel sorry for me, Lynne. I'm just grateful for modern medicine. If I had been born a hundred years ago, I wouldn't have made it past thirteen."

"Is that when you got it?"

Joe nodded. "Yeah, I started getting sick the summer I was twelve. Since two of my cousins have it also, nobody was too surprised. Or too upset, for that matter. Thank goodness, nobody ever felt sorry for me, or tried to baby me. Mom just put me on the diet and gave me the shots until I could do it for myself."

"Smart mom," Lynne said.

"Yes, she was."

Joe went on to tell Lynne funny stories about his family, speaking fondly of them. Lynne knew that she and Joe were going to have to talk about their argument last night, but she was glad of a short reprieve before they did so.

"Thanks for dinner," Joe said, getting up from the table. "May I at least help you with the dishes?"

"Are you sure you feel all right?" Lynne asked.

"The food and the nap worked wonders," Joe said. "I probably feel better than you do. You didn't sleep much last night, did you?"

"No, I didn't," Lynne said shortly. She carried the plates to the kitchen, and they cleaned up the mess from the party as well as the dishes from tonight. Joe was silent, wondering whether Lynne would level with him on why she didn't like his friends, and Lynne dreaded admitting to Joe that his friends had laughed about her looks. When Lynne had put the last of the dishes away, Joe took her hand and led her out to the living room. He motioned for her to sit down on the couch and sat down next to her, not letting go of her hand. "Lynne, after you left last night I got to thinking. It just isn't like you to decide that you don't like someone, or a group of people, especially after you've knocked yourself out to entertain

115

them. What happened, Lynne? What happened to turn you off to my friends?"

Lynne sat silent for a moment, biting her lip. "Come on , Lynne, talk to me," Joe pleaded. "I know I said they were great, because to me they always have been. But that doesn't mean that some of them aren't capable of unkindness on occasion. What happened? Did someone criticize the party?"

"No, they loved the party," Lynne said dryly. "Even I could tell that. It was the way they looked at me when they found out that you were dating me. Like you'd taken leave of your senses."

"Oh." Joe shrugged. "I guess they don't think you're the type of woman I dated in Dallas."

Lynne pulled her hand away from Joe's and stood up, turning her back to him. "And I'm not, am I? You dated pretty women back in Dallas."

Joe sat quietly for a moment. "I never thought about it. Yes, I guess I dated mostly pretty women in Dallas."

"That's what I thought."

"But they weren't all raving beauties, if that's what you're thinking. And I sure didn't ask them out just because they were pretty."

"I didn't think you did," Lynne said, turning around. "But it hurt, Joe, knowing that I don't hold a candle to the women you usually date." Her eyes became moist and she blinked back tears. "And it hurt when they looked at me like I was some kind of side-show freak."

"They didn't do that," Joe said. "I'm sorry they were surprised at first. Some of it might have been because you're taller than me. Tall women always intimidated me before, and some of them knew it. That's probably why

116

they were surprised, Lynne. It didn't have anything to do with your face or your figure."

"Sure," Lynne said bitterly. "And that's of course why Sharon Kovaks and one of the others were laughing about your horse-faced girlfriend."

Joe couldn't hide the wince. "Lynne, I'm sorry. Sharon's always been catty, but I honestly didn't realize she could be that cruel."

Lynne's smile was sad. "She was being cruel, but she was being truthful. She had no idea that I would overhear her, or I'm sure she would never have said it." She turned her back to stare out the window at the deepening dusk. "It just hurts, sometimes, Joe, always being laughed at because I'm ugly."

"Lynne, you're not ugly!" Joe said. He leapt off the couch and stood behind her, his hands on her arms. "You're a very lovely woman."

Lynne pulled away from him. "Oh, don't lie to me, Joe. Can you honestly look me in the eye and tell me I'm pretty? Did you give me a second look that day I delivered the calf for you? Well, did you?"

Joe was silent for a moment. "No, I can't look you in the eye and tell you that you're pretty. I didn't say you're a pretty woman, Lynne. I said you're a lovely woman. And there's a big difference between the two. A pretty woman, by an accident of birth, has her facial features arranged just right. She might be as mean as the devil, selfish and grasping, and cold, but she's got a pretty face. So what? A lovely woman, on the other hand, would make a special trip out here to bring Carlos papers for his sister, work like the devil to give a party for a group of strangers, and help a sick man round up his stray cattle even when she's mad at him."

"Whoopee," Lynne said sarcastically as she sat back down on the couch.

Joe pulled up the hassock and sat down across from her. "And to answer your second question, I most certainly did notice you both the first and the second time you came out here." He grinned a little sheepishly. "You intimidated the hell out of me."

"I did?" Lynne asked.

"You sure did, lady. You towered over me, and you knew what to do to save my cow!"

"But you didn't notice me as a woman," Lynne said softly. "And that's what hurts, Joe."

"I did that night, Lynne. And I almost asked you for your phone number, but I thought you probably already had a long-legged boyfriend someplace."

"You would have asked anyway, if I'd been pretty," Lynne said. "Joe, you don't realize how it feels. You're handsome, and you have no idea what it's like to not be attractive. It matters in this world what you look like, Joe. It matters a lot."

Joe thought a minute. "Why?"

"I don't know how to explain it, but it does," Lynne argued. "Look at the way your friends reacted to me."

"I don't think it matters to most people, Lynne, that you're not a raving beauty," Joe said. "It doesn't matter to me. If it did, I wouldn't still be around, now, would I?"

Lynne shrugged. "Maybe you like my cooking."

"And maybe I like your company. And maybe I like arguing with you, and the way you laugh. And maybe I'm very, very attracted to you, even if your face and your figure aren't perfect."

118

"I'll buy the first three, but you can forget the last one," Lynne scoffed.

Joe raised one eyebrow. "Then why did I get such a bang out of the peep show yesterday afternoon? You left the bathroom door open a crack while you were drying your hair, and by the time you were through I was ready to ravish you. Would have, too, if we hadn't had guests coming in a half hour."

Lynne looked dubious. "I'll admit that there's quite a bit of attraction between us—at least there has been on my part—but you simply can't convince me that I'm attractive enough to turn a man on."

"Bet I can," Joe said softly. Before Lynne knew what he was doing, he was on the couch beside her and had his arms around her. His lips explored hers, softly at first, then with tantalizing firmness. Lynne groaned as his arms came around her and held her tightly to him. Lynne's arms slowly crept around Joe's neck, and her hands roamed through his soft blond hair. Joe's kiss deepened, his tongue forcing open her lips and plundering the sweetness he found within. Her breathing coming in passionate gasps, Lynne felt herself sliding down into the soft cushions of the sofa. Joe kissed her slowly and thoroughly before he raised his head. "Lynne, you do have the looks to turn a man on," he said, his eyes glazed with passion. "I wanted you so badly that day on the boat, the first time I saw you in a bikini, it was all I could do not to take you then, right out in the middle of the bay. I've wanted you every single time we've been together. Hundreds of times I've pictured what you might look like without your clothes on, and every single time I've been turned on by what I saw."

"You *like* skinny legs and a visible rib cage?" Lynne asked in astonishment.

Joe covered her lips in a warm, erotic kiss. "Yes, I do like your long legs that go on forever," he said as he pulled away from her. He placed gentle fingers on her rib cage. "And I do like your soft, vulnerable middle, and your tiny waist and the flat tummy that goes below it, and your pretty little breasts that turn up just a smidgen on the ends."

"But I'm not beautiful like those other women," Lynne protested quietly.

"No, you're not. You look like Lynne, and Lynne turns me on very much." His lips, as he spoke, nibbled the side of her neck. "I want to make love to Lynne. No one else, not one of the pretty women I left behind in Dallas." His lips traveled lower, caressing her neck before drifting down to the tender flesh below. "I wanted this Lynne so much I went out and got something to protect her, so I could make love to her if she would have me." He raised his head and gazed into her slumberous eyes. "How about it, Lynne? Will you become my lover tonight?"

Lynne shrugged helplessly. "I may disappoint you," she said. "You're used to such beautiful lov—"

Joe cut off her protest with a hard, punishing kiss that left Lynne breathless. "Forget the other lovers I've had," he said harshly. "And I'll forget yours. I want you tonight, Lynne. Not some centerfold or a china doll."

"I want you, too, Joe," Lynne said. "I want you like I've never wanted a man before in my life. Not that there have been many," she admitted.

"I haven't had all that many either," Joe surprised her by saying. "I could have seen a lot more action in Dallas if I had wanted to. So don't worry about disappointing me, Lynne. I don't think you could do that if you tried." He pushed aside the fabric of her top and caressed her breast above the cup of her silky black bra, sending shivers of delight down to Lynne's toes.

Lynne wound her arms around Joe's waist and held herself to him, the evidence of his body convincing her that he did want her tonight. He pressed her down into the sofa, the scratchy fabric of his jeans a pleasant friction against the soft skin of her legs. Lynne moaned helplessly and tried to shift her body so that she and Joe would be even more intimately entwined, but hit her knee on the coffee table and cried out softly.

"Poor knee," Joe said and he reached down and rubbed it. He slid down to place a tender kiss on her knee and banged the small of his back against the same coffee table. "Ow! That hurts!" He pushed the coffee table back and sat back on his heels, his sexy eyes taking in the sensual abandon on Lynne's thoroughly kissed face. "I don't know about you, but I think we're both too big to finish this on the couch." He rose to his feet and extended his hand to Lynne. "My bed's big and comfortable, and it's been lonely lately."

Lynne swung to her feet and let Joe lead her by the hand to his bedroom. With a quick motion he turned back the covers on his king-sized bed and almost shyly sat down and patted a place for her beside him. Lynne sat down next to him and kicked off her sandals. "Undress me," she whispered. "I've dreamed of having you take my clothes off."

"My pleasure," Joe said, and his trembling fingers pulled her top over her head. He placed quick, tantalizing kisses along the edge of her bra before unsnapping the front closure and gently removing it. "The better to taste you with, my dear," he teased as his tongue darted forward and tantalized one exposed peak.

"I want to touch you too," Lynne said, and her eager fingers unbuttoned the front of Joe's shirt and pushed it off his shoulders. "I love to do this"—running her fingers through the soft hair of his chest.

"You have all night to do that," Joe said, and he bore her down into the sheets. His mouth closed over one nipple and he suckled it gently, his teeth and his tongue working erotic magic on her tender bud.

"Ooh, I love it when you touch me there," Lynne whimpered. Her lower body shifted restlessly beneath his. Joe continued to suckle her breasts as his hands drifted lower, unzipping her shorts. In one smooth motion he stripped the shorts and panties from her body, leaving her naked to his eager gaze.

Lynne was suddenly consumed by overwhelming shyness. "Turn off the light," she pleaded.

"No way am I going to turn off the light," Joe said firmly. "Half my pleasure is looking at you, didn't you know that?" His gaze traveled down her body, and Lynne could see the evidence of his growing desire for her. "You're even more beautiful in the nude than I thought you would be," he said as his hand touched the most feminine part of her anatomy.

Lynne gazed into Joe's eyes for a moment before she pushed him down into the sheets. She unzipped his jeans and drew them and his shorts most of the way down, and Joe kicked them off altogether, leaving himself naked and unashamed in front of her. "You really are beautiful," Lynne breathed. She took in the symmetry of Joe's body, the strong lines complementing the perfection in his face. With a feather-light touch Lynne ran her hand down him, past his chest and waist to the sinewed strength of his hips. She lingered there a moment, shyly touching him intimately before her fingers traveled lower, down his hair-roughened thighs to one knee. Joe grasped her shoulders and pulled her down beside him, showering her neck and her shoulders and her breasts with hot, moist kisses.

Lynne returned kiss for kiss, caress for caress, touch for touch. As Joe's lips caressed her breasts, his hands drifted lower, finding and touching the sweetness of her femininity until she was ready to cry out with pleasure. When he sensed that she was near the brink, he tensed and pulled away from her. Lynne started to protest, but when she saw that Joe had only paused to protect her, she helped him prepare himself for the act of love, her gentle fingers accomplishing what his trembling ones couldn't.

Joe pushed Lynne down into the bed and covered her body with his own. "Are you ready for me?" he asked. When Lynne nodded, he parted her legs and made them one. Lynne gasped a little at the intimacy of his possession, pleasure and delight suffusing her being as Joe started to move within her. Slowly at first, savoring the reality of their togetherness, Joe stroked and caressed, gently moving over Lynne with a rhythm as old as time itself. Lynne gave herself up to his passionate embrace, her legs winding themselves around his waist as he moved within her. When he sensed that she was ready, his motions increased in speed and intensity, the flames of passion licking them as their level of excitement grew higher and higher.

Lynne matched Joe move for move, her hands caressing, her hips rocking with his. She felt the excitement spiraling within her, excitement and tension such as she had never known before. Faster and faster, higher and higher, Lynne did not know how much more she could stand, and when the storm broke within her, she cried out softly. Hearing her expression of delight, Joe released the tight hold on his own emotions and let himself be overtaken with the same kind of pleasure he had just given Lynne, a cry on his own lips revealing to her just how much she had given him.

Joe turned over on his side and held Lynne so that she faced him. His gentle fingers brushed the hair from her forehead. "I knew it would be beautiful with you, Lynne, but I hadn't guessed how beautiful," he admitted.

"I've never known anything like that either," Lynne said.

Joe tipped her face so that he could give her a long, lingering kiss. "I don't want you ever to think you're undesirable," he said. "You're the most desirable woman I've ever known."

"Thank you," Lynne said, cradling his body against the warmth of hers.

"What time should I set the alarm for?" he asked. "How much time do you need to get to work on time?"

"Set it early." She made a face.

He set the alarm. "We'll get plenty of sleep—it's still early." He settled back down beside Lynne, pillowing his head between her breasts. "Do you mind? I've dreamed of sleeping with you this way for a long time."

"I like it," Lynne admitted, putting her arms around Joe and cradling him close to her. She shut her eyes against the sting of happy tears. She had been wrong—she was physically attractive to Joe. And that made her very happy.

But could she inspire his love? Did she need to be pretty to do that? Physical attraction was one thing—falling in love with a woman was quite a different story. She knew that she was falling in love with Joe, if she hadn't already, and she had always dreamed of having a man fall in love with her, deeply and romantically. Did she dare hope that Joe might grow to love her someday? She just didn't know if she had what it took to inspire Joe's love, but her last thought as she drifted off to sleep was that she certainly hoped she did.

Joe raised himself a little and gazed down into Lynne's sleeping face, the light from the dim bedside lamp illuminating her features gently in the dark of the night. It was early yet, and Joe had slept awhile this afternoon, so he got out of bed, careful not to wake Lynne, and sat in the wing chair beside the bed, studying her face in repose. She wasn't very pretty, but he didn't care at all. And he had been surprised tonight to learn that it bothered her—he had assumed that she hadn't cared either. But he had learned tonight that she was very sensitive about what she considered an important lacking.

Joe sighed in the darkness. He would gladly trade places with her or any other ordinary-looking person any day, if they would take the diabetes along with his pretty face. Although he put on a brave, cheerful, accepting front for the world, there were days like today he hated having diabetes, and despised being tied to a clock and a diet. He hadn't had ice cream since he was twelve years old and had never had a drink in his life, for all the time he had spent in discos and nightspots. He would love to have gotten drunk once, just to see how it felt.

Joe pushed aside his thoughts of self-pity and looked at Lynne again. She just didn't know her own worth. Any woman who would take care of him and his runaway cows after the way he had treated her last night—she had to be one in a million. And Joe realized that he had fallen in love with his one-in-a-million woman. He wanted desperately to spend the rest of his life with the woman who slept in his bed tonight. He wanted to marry her, to sleep with her every night, to kiss her good-bye every morning when she left for work, to watch her swell with his children. He wanted to grow old with her, to watch her hair grow gray and to sit on the porch swing with her when they were too old to do anything else.

Joe stretched his legs out in front of him. But would she want to go through life with a runt two inches shorter than she was? Joe laughed at himself for even thinking about his height. His worrying about it was going to do about as much good as her worrying about her face. Besides, Lynne had never seemed to mind that he was shorter than she. But he still felt a little inadequate because of it.

Absently Joe rubbed the vein where he had given himself his insulin injection this morning. He wasn't really worried about the height difference, but Lynne's reaction to his having diabetes did have him concerned. She had been great this afternoon when he had gotten sick, but would she want to live with him on a permanent basis, knowing he could have a problem at any time? Would she want to run the risk of her children or her grandchildren having diabetes? Or would she rather marry a man who was completely healthy?

Joe turned out the light and crawled back into bed beside Lynne, stretching himself out next to her long, soft body. *Please, God, let her learn to love me,* he prayed into the darkness of the room. Please let her not care about the diabetes. Let her not care that I'm not perfect.

CHAPTER SEVEN

Lynne blinked at the strange buzzing, wondering in her sleepy state why the alarm clock sounded so funny. She stretched out her arm to punch it off and encountered another arm reaching for the same place. Her eyes flew open, and Lynne watched as Joe found the alarm button and turned it off without opening his eyes. "Neat trick," she said sleepily. "I have to look at mine."

"Ah, well, some of us have talent and some of us don't," Joe said, pulling Lynne close and covering her lips in a scorching kiss, still not opening his eyes. "Like me, for instance." He left her mouth and nibbled his way down her neck. "I can find your neck"—he gently caressed the soft skin of her neck with his lips and his tongue—"and your shoulder"—his lips drifted lower, finding and kissing the tender skin of her shoulders—"and I can even find these," he murmured, his lips closing over one of Lynne's nipples and tormenting it lovingly. "All without opening my eyes." He raised his head and grinned at her impudently, his eyes opening finally to gaze at her with hooded sensuality. "But I prefer making love to you with my eyes open. Do we have time?"

Lynne squinted at the clock in the early-morning gray. "Good grief, Joe, I said early, not the dead of night." She wrapped her arms around him and pulled his face close to hers. "Make love to me, cowboy," she whispered, raising her lips for another good-morning kiss.

Joe lowered his head and covered her mouth in a kiss that was deep and inviting. Moaning a little, Lynne opened to him, meeting him boldly as he gained entrance to her sweetness. For long minutes they clung together and caressed one another, the weight of Joe's body warm and comfortable on Lynne's. His hands touched her shoulders and arms, his lips found the sweetness of her cheeks, her nose, her eyelids. He wound his fingers into the long hair that had become tangled in the night, anchoring her gently so that he could explore each and every contour of her face with his tender passion. "Joe, Joe, I—" Words failed her, and she gave herself up to Joe's erotic lovemaking.

"We waited too long for this," Joe said. He caressed her back with gentle fingers. "We should have become lovers weeks ago."

"Yes, we should have," Lynne agreed, and she found and stroked the strength in Joe's back and shoulders. "We've missed out on some good loving."

"Let's make up for it, then," Joe said. "We'll do this as often as we're together." He dipped his head and nibbled the small bud of her breast with his lips, chuckling when she swelled with passion.

"We'll scare the horses," Lynne teased. Her fingers found one of Joe's flat male nipples.

"So what? Maybe they need lessons." Joe laughed.

Lynne turned him around so that he was lying on his back. "Let me give you some of the pleasure you gave me." Her lips started at his neck, touching and tasting, and worked their way down his hard, warm shoulder to the softness of his chest. "You're soft and hard at the same time," she said, rubbing her cheek against the velvet strength she found. Her lips found one nipple in the dense tangle and she took it into her mouth, flicking her tongue back and forth until it was hard to the touch.

"Lord, woman, did you take lessons or something?" Joe moaned. Her lips now tantalized his other nipple.

"Yes, I did," Lynne murmured, her eyes dancing. "I took lessons from a good-looking blond cowboy. Took 'em last night, in fact. That's why I remember so much."

"Show me what else you remember," Joe murmured.

Lynne's hands slid down him, touching and caressing him until he was squirming with unleashed passion. He stroked the skin of her waist and stomach, his fingers evoking tremors of delight as they made their way lower, rubbing the smoothness of her slender hips. Boldly, Joe found the center of her femininity and caressed it with the tip of his finger until Lynne could stand no more of his teasing. She applied the protective device herself before moving herself over Joe and joining their bodies in one sure stroke.

Joe gasped with both pleasure and surprise as Lynne made them one. Her boldness pleased and surprised him; he encouraged her to set the pace of their lovemaking, his hands resting lightly on her hips, helping, not guiding. Not bound by the shyness and caution that had marked their lovemaking last night, Lynne arched her back and gave full rein to the passion that swept through her, carrying Joe along with her on a searing tide. Joe went eagerly, welcoming Lynne's sensual lovemaking and reveling in it as she gave herself to him; and yet she was taking, too, greedily helping herself to the delight Joe offered her. Her hair bounced around her face in a wild tangle, and she gave and took and shared until the two of them were swept away together, transported to an exploding world of ecstasy. They reached the height of passion as one, their mutual cries of delight a joyous sound in the early-morning dawn.

Lynne collapsed against Joe; his arms wrapped around her and held her to him. "I thought last night was wonderful, but that was—well . . ." Joe stroked Lynne's hair and held her until their breathing had slowed to normal. "I've never had a woman really make love to me before," he mused, kissing her temple. "It was beautiful."

"I loved it," Lynne said. She glanced at the clock. "But I'd really better get up now. I'm supposed to be at work in an hour and a half." She got out of bed and reached for the clothes she had taken off last night.

"I washed and dried the clothes you left here Saturday night," Joe said. "Why don't you take a shower with me before you go?"

Lynne surveyed Joe's naked body with bold admiration. "I'd love to, if you think we'll get out of the shower before noon."

Joe pointed toward the shower. "I think you're safe for the next ten minutes."

Lynne walked past Joe and patted him on the bottom. "I know I am, but what about you?"

Joe followed her into the bathroom and got into the shower with Lynne. He adjusted the temperature of the water and handed Lynne her own washcloth. They shared the spray and a bar of soap, rubbing suds on each other's naked body and becoming aroused again in the process. Joe squirted soap in Lynne's hair and scrubbed it into a fine lather. Lynne teased Joe about her being eye level with his future bald spot, kissing the imaginary thinning of his hair. They clowned around while they rinsed the soap out of their hair and wrapped their dripping bodies in thick bath towels.

Lynne dried herself and blotted her hair, helping herself to Joe's deodorant and an extra toothbrush she found in the drawer. Joe returned wearing a pair of Jockey shorts and carrying Lynne's clothes. "I don't know how to thank you for yesterday," he said as Lynne dressed. "You helped me so much."

"Except for you getting sick and scaring me, I enjoyed it," she said as she got out the hair drier. She adjusted the setting and started sectioning her hair. "How did the cows get out, anyway?"

"That bull of mine stomped down that flimsy fence along the road," Joe said. "Uncle Jack put it up in the days he ran smaller cattle that didn't need a very strong fence."

"Yeah, I know. When daddy bought his first Brangus, he had to add another wire all the way around. Say, I bet you need to do that. One more wire along the top will keep Romeo in."

"Yeah, I know, but I just haven't gotten that far. The foreman's good on supervising, but a little short on real work, and I had to let half the workers go to pay him." He lathered his face with shaving cream and Lynne moved over to give him room at the mirror.

"You're working yourself to death," Lynne said disapprovingly. "It's a wonder you have time to see me."

"I make time to see you," Joe admitted. "As busy as I am, I just can't neglect what we have together."

Lynne leaned down and kissed the tip of his nose, careful to miss the shaving cream and his razor. "Are you too

131

proud to accept some help until you're back on your feet?"

"Oh, Lynne, I couldn't borrow money from you," Joe said. "This place may be years away from seeing a profit."

"I offered you help, not money," Lynne said. "I grew up on a ranch, and since I've started going with you, I realize just how much I miss the life. I could move in here for a week or two and help you for a few hours when I get home from work. How about it?"

"I hate for you to come out here and work after you've put in a full day," he objected.

"I wouldn't mind. I miss the ranch, Joe. Honestly. And besides, you made time for me when you didn't have it. Why can't I give you some time I do have?"

Joe wiped his face and put his arms around Lynne. "You have to be the most generous woman in the county," he said. "Yes, I'll accept your help, gladly. What do you know how to do?"

"Just about anything you need."

"Well, you can take your choice. I need to put up an extra wire on the fence—all the way around—I haven't mowed all the pastures yet, I need to vaccinate about half the herd, and if I decide to castrate I need to do that. What do you think about castrating? I've asked around, and most are castrating but a few have stopped."

"I don't know," Lynne said. She turned off the drier. "Now, I can do just about anything you mentioned. Would you like me to help with the vaccinating? I used to be pretty good at that."

"Sure, that would be great," Joe said. He opened the drawer where he kept his insulin and swiftly gave himself his morning injection. As he eased the needle from his arm, he remembered Lynne and searched her face, looking for any sign of distaste or rejection.

Lynne whistled under her breath. "Tell you what. I'll do the fences or the mowing. I think you have the vaccinating down pat."

Joe laughed with relief that his shot had not bothered her. "I sure wouldn't want to get that huge shot I have to give them."

"Joe, I've got to go now, but I'll be back this evening as soon as I get some clothes packed," Lynne said, her eyes sparkling at the thought of a week or two here with Joe, doing the outdoor work she loved so much. She kissed him good-bye and half ran, half skipped, to her car.

Joe stood at the window and watched Lynne drive away. She had been tickled that he had accepted her offer to help him. And he could tell that it wasn't just a desire to be with him—she was honestly looking forward to spending some time working outside. He hadn't realized until now how much she missed the ranch she'd grown up on. Her offer was a real blessing, and Joe had no doubt that she would help him a lot in the next week or two. He glanced at the rumpled sheets and grinned wickedly. But if he had his way about it, they would do more in the next two weeks than just work!

Lynne carried her suitcases into Joe's living room. She had packed enough to last her over a week, and without batting an eye had given Ben Miller Joe's number, in case of an emergency. Ben made it a practice not to interfere in the private lives of his agents, but he had grinned and winked at her as he wrote down the telephone number. Laura had giggled like a schoolgirl and had promised to cover for her if their old-fashioned mother asked why

Lynne wasn't home when she called. Lynne changed out of her uniform into an ancient pair of jeans and a work-shirt. Joe was nowhere to be found, but she had spotted Carlos struggling to put up another row of barbed wire at the top of the fence posts. He was having trouble, and his colorful Spanish expletives could be heard all the way to the gate.

Lynne drove the pickup across the pasture. "Need some help?" she asked Carlos in Spanish.

"Please! I'm no good at this." He gestured to the scratches on his arms. "If Consuela weren't depending on me for money, I'd take off this afternoon and find a *cantina!*"

"All you would get out of that is a headache," Lynne said. She took the roll of wire from Carlos and uncoiled a section, careful not to catch her skin on the barbs. She positioned the wire at the correct height and Carlos nailed it in. "How's Consuela?" she asked as she unrolled more wire and backed down the fence.

"She still doesn't have a job, but she's able to feed her children with what I give her. *El jefe* gave me some money to take her to buy them clothes. That was good of him."

Lynne wasn't surprised. "Yes, that was good of Joe," she agreed. She and Carlos worked for nearly three hours, until the sun started to go down on them, and made considerable progress on the fence.

Joe had eaten supper already and was scraping his plate when Lynne came in. "Where were you? I saw your car but then you weren't around."

"Carlos and I were working on the fence by the high-way," Lynne said. "Save any for me?"

134

Joe took a covered plate from the oven. "I had to go on and eat. Sorry."

"I understand, believe me," Lynne assured him. "Oh, this smells delicious!" She ate her steak and vegetables and sliced herself a big piece of the cake she had brought. "I hate to eat this in front of you, but I need the calories," she apologized.

"I'll take it out on your voodoo doll," Joe said.

"You mean if I start to feel these funny pains—"

"That's right, I'm paying you back," Joe teased, planting a kiss on the top of her head. "The only thing I'm worrying about is going broke feeding you."

Lynne took a long, hot bath, then put on a satiny flowered nightgown and stood at the door, staring out into the peaceful night. "Come on out, Lynne," Joe said. "It's beautiful out here."

"I'm not dressed," Lynne protested.

"Turn off the porch light. They can't really see you from the cabins or the highway, anyway."

Lynne turned off the light and sat down next to Joe on the porch swing. He took her hand in his, and together they gazed up at the sparkling expanse of stars that blanketed the sky. "I never could see the Milky Way in Dallas," Joe said softly.

"You can't even see it in town," Lynne said. "It's so beautiful out here! You're a lucky man, Joe. You have so much of what really matters."

Joe gazed at Lynne's upturned face, and his heart swelled with love for the woman beside him. "Yes, Lynne, I have a lot of what really matters. I have more than you realize." He kissed her cheek tenderly and squeezed her hand, and they stared up at the sky for a few more minutes before they went inside and made passionate love.

"Joe! Joe, I'm here," Lynne called as she loped into the barn and skidded to a halt. Joe was kneeling in one of the mare's stalls, intently watching Josie strain to deliver her foal. Lynne leaned over and put her hand on Joe's shoulder. "She isn't in any trouble," she said softly. "That foal will be here in a few minutes."

"Oh, I didn't think she was," Joe said, pulling Lynne down beside him. "It's just that I've been here five months, and I haven't gotten over the miracle of birth yet."

Lynne smiled. "You won't. I saw it every day of my life growing up, and it's still just as beautiful to me now as it was the first time I saw it. Look, here comes the hoof!"

They watched in silence and in awe as Josie's foal emerged. "Oh, look, it's a little colt," Lynne cooed. "He's precious." The colt was chocolate-brown with a white star on his forehead.

"Why don't you name him for me?" Joe asked.

Lynne thought a minute. "How about Marshmallow? You know he's brown like cocoa and has a marshmallow."

"Marshmallow it is," Joe said. He and Lynne took care of the mare's needs and forked her a little more hay. The colt, with a little nudging from his mother, stood up on spindly legs and wobbled around the stall. "Isn't that faster than they usually get up?" Joe asked.

"A little," Lynne said. "That little horse is a winner. Gonna keep him?"

"Probably," Joe said. "If I have to, I'll sell that mean

old gelding and keep this one. I don't like that horse one bit!"

"Good idea," Lynne agreed. "So what do you need me to do today?"

"How about helping me with that last section of fence?" Joe asked. "I can't believe that I'm almost caught up. You've been an unbelievable amount of help."

"I've enjoyed it," Lynne said, picking up a roll of barbed wire.

"Even getting kicked by that bull calf?" Joe teased. One of the earliest spring bulls had gotten big enough to kick with a wallop, and Lynne's shin still sported a huge bruise from his well-placed hoof.

"All right, I enjoyed most of it," Lynne amended. "And you did a great job of kissing it better."

"I did, didn't I?" Joe grinned. Lynne tossed the wire into the back of the pickup and they bounced across the pasture to the last section of fence that needed strengthening. Joe glanced at the woman beside him, noticing that her expression these days was almost always open, not unreadable as it had been when he had first met her. She had been here for almost two weeks, pitching in after she got off work and putting in a day that would kill most people, but the demanding schedule suited her just fine. She had admitted one night, as they snuggled close after making love, that for the first time in a long time she felt really challenged, and that she was going to be at loose ends for a while after she moved back to her apartment.

But did she have to go back? Joe pushed his sunglasses back up on his nose. Clearly she had enjoyed her two weeks with him. She was always smiling, and humming under her breath while cooking him breakfast or sharing the supper he had prepared, or sat together on the big porch swing. Would she like to live here on a permanent basis?

"There's where Carlos and I left off yesterday," Lynne said, pointing to a post about halfway down the fence that bordered the Michaels place.

"Y'all got even farther than I realized," Joe admitted. "We can have this finished by suppertime." He unloaded the wire from the back of the pickup. "I guess there won't be much more work for you to help me with," he said casually, watching Lynne's face closely for a reaction.

"Yes, I guess that's true," she said, her eyes wistful. "I'll have to move back home."

"Yeah," Joe mumbled, ducking his head to hide the satisfied expression on his face. Lynne had looked disappointed that she had to go back to her apartment. Good. That meant she liked it here, and that she might be willing to stay.

Lynne tried to hide her sadness as she worked beside Joe. She had loved the last two weeks here with him, and not just because of the ranch. Her eyes feasted on him, his disreputable straw hat pushed to the back of his head as he nailed in the barbed wire. He was hot and grimy, and his boots were run down and scruffy. His slick friends from Dallas wouldn't know him like this, but to Lynne he had never looked more appealing. She had fallen in love with Joe and had admitted it to herself days ago. She loved him deeply and dearly, with all the passion and excitement of the most beautiful of romantic novels. But she loved him realistically too. She knew that he snored, and that he was cross at times from the insulin, and that sometimes he chafed at his dietary restrictions. And she loved him in spite of his shortcomings, as well as for his strengths.

Lynne unrolled the wire for Joe and backed to the next fence post, grinning when he looked up and winked at her in that sexy way of his. He had made love to her every night since she had moved in, and Lynne now knew beyond a shadow of a doubt that she had what it took to inspire his passion. She and Joe had taken each other to earth-shattering heights that Lynne hadn't ever dreamed existed. Even if Joe stopped seeing her, she would never again doubt her own sensuality, or her ability to please a man. But did Joe's feelings for her ever go beyond the physical? Had he fallen in love with her, the way she had fallen in love with him? She didn't know, but she hoped so as she thought of how wonderful it would be.

They finished the fence and shared a warm shower before Lynne fixed them a simple dinner of hamburgers and fruit. While Joe did some of his paperwork, she wandered down to the barn to check on Josie and Marshmallow. The newborn was resting in the straw, his sleepy eyes and his bulging tummy telling his story. Lynne held out a lump of sugar to Josie. "You're a good girl," she crooned as Josie nibbled from her outstretched palm.

"Here, horse, you better remember who pays your feed bill," Joe said, holding out his own sugar cube. "I thought you might be out here." He curved his arm around Lynne's waist. "He's doing fine, isn't he?"

"Just super," Lynne said, leaning into the warmth of Joe's body. "I'll have to come see him a lot after I've gone home."

"When are you going?" Joe asked. He hoped his voice sounded casual.

"I can help you get that last pasture mowed tomorrow,

and I guess I'd better move out after that. Laura said that mother was suspicious. I'm going to miss it here, though."

They watched Marshmallow for a few minutes before they went back to the house. Lynne relaxed on the king-sized bed and watched a television movie, and Joe sat outside in the porch swing, staring out at the pastures dappled by the glow of an almost full moon. He loved this ranch, every square inch, every tree, every cow and calf, and before Lynne had come to stay he had been perfectly content. But now he had to admit that his beloved ranch would be horribly lonely once Lynne had gone home.

Joe propped his foot on the swing and mulled over the question that had haunted him for the last two weeks. Would Lynne marry him and share his life out here? She had never directly said that she loved him, but she treated him as if she did, in and out of bed. And she did love the ranching life. But she knew that he had an essentially incurable disease—a treatable one, certainly, but a disease he would have for the rest of his life. And he was fairly sure she knew that his children would have a chance of inheriting it. Would that put her off marrying him?

He had to take a chance and ask her, even if she said no. He loved her too much, and wanted to be with her too badly, not at least to ask her to be his wife. A slow, warm smile spread across Joe's face as he thought of how he would ask Lynne to marry him. She would have a proposal she would never forget as long as she lived!

Lynne put the last of her freshly laundered jeans into her suitcase and wedged a stack of neatly folded panties

140

into one corner. "I guess that about does it," she said shutting the suitcase. "I'll put it in the car tomorrow when I go to work."

Joe watched her from the wing chair, one leg crossed over the other. "Would you like to go for one last ride before you move back to your place?" he asked. "It's a beautiful night, and it seems like a shame to waste it in the house."

"Sure," Lynne said, perking up a little at the thought of a nighttime ride. The sun was just setting in a red ball of fury in the west, and at the same time a silvery-bright full moon was rising in the east. It was a delightful evening for a moonlight ride. "I'll put on a pair of jeans." Totally unselfconscious in front of Joe, she changed from her shorts to a pair of the jeans she had just packed.

They saddled the horses together, and Joe tied a mysterious-looking pack to the back of his saddle. The light of dusk was fading, but the bright silver of the moonlight glazed everything. "I think I like this time of day best," Lynne said as she guided Joe's horse Roper away from the barn. "Everything's so peaceful now."

"You don't like dawn the best?" Joe asked. "That's become my favorite, now that I have to get up early."

"No, I'll stick with dusk," Lynne said. They didn't say much as they rode, and Lynne sensed that Joe had something on his mind. She started to question him, but decided not to pry, and instead let herself soak up the peace and beauty of the hot summer night. A warm wind, faintly tinged with salt, blew in from the southeast, stirring the tendrils of hair at Lynne's temple. She would miss this when she moved back to town tomorrow, but she would come out and see Joe often, just as often as he

141

asked her to. And she would continue to love him and hope that someday he would feel the same way she felt.

Joe took the lead and guided them deep into the south pasture, far away from the highway or a bordering fence. They had ridden past small groups of cattle, some of which stared at them for a minute before returning to their rest, but this part of the pasture was deserted. Joe pointed out a stand of trees straddling a creek bed. "There's something there I want to show you," he said. Lynne nodded and together they rode into the grove.

They crossed the dry creek bed and Joe reined his horse. "Tie your horse here. We have to walk a few yards."

Joe took her by the hand and led her a few yards through the trees to a small clearing. "I used to come and dig up the weeds every summer," Joe said as Lynne stared at the two old tombstones, their inscriptions barely visible in the dim moonlight. "I thought they deserved better than to be overgrown."

"Who were they?" Lynne asked. "Your grandparents?"

"My great-great-grandparents," Joe explained. "They both died before the turn of the century. I just thought you might like seeing a beautiful spot."

"I do," Lynne said. Joe told her about the couple and then they wandered back to where the horses were tied. But instead of untying the horses, Joe took the pack off his saddle. "What's that?" Lynne asked.

"I thought you might like a moonlight picnic." He unrolled an old quilt and spread it out in a patch of grass.

"Why, Joe, I'd love one." She sat down across from him on the quilt. He opened a sack and withdrew two peaches, a cluster of grapes, cheese, bread, and two soft-drink cans.

Joe ripped the tab from one can and handed it to her. "I wish it were wine," he said as he gave her one of the peaches.

"This is nectar and ambrosia," Lynne said, biting into the juicy peach. Joe sat down beside her and nibbled on a grape. Lynne was fully tuned in to the sensations of the night—the warm wind, the smell of the grass beneath her, the sweetness of the fruit she ate, the searing sensuality of the man at her side. She turned so that the wind blew straight into her face, and breathed deeply.

"Allow me," Joe said. He held her hand up to his lips and began to lick the stickiness of the peach from her fingers. His soft mouth nibbled and touched as he did his cleansing work, the unexpected intimacy causing Lynne to shiver with pleasure. Inch by inch, finger by finger, he cleansed her hand, and dropped it to pick up the other.

"I didn't get anything on that one," Lynne whispered.

"So what?" Joe asked, and he bathed her clean hand in the same kind of sensual torment as he had the other one. His lips velvet, he caressed her until she was trembling.

"Are you doing what I think you're doing?" Lynne asked as Joe reached for the cluster of grapes.

"Probably." Gently, he parted her lips with a seedless grape. "Unless you're afraid of scaring the horses."

Lynne pulled a grape from the cluster and put it into Joe's mouth. "I don't think we'll scare them too badly, do you?" she asked.

Joe shook his head. He broke off another grape and fed it to Lynne. Back and forth they fed one another, their fingers gently caressing each other's lips. Lynne's eyes were heavy with passion by the time Joe had fed her the last one. Her breathing slightly uneven, she touched the small triangle at the base of his throat. "I want you, Lynne," he said, his voice vibrating through her finger. He put his hands on her shoulders. "I've never loved a woman the way I love you."

Lynne froze, and stared at Joe. "You love me?" she whispered. "You really love me?"

"Yes, Lynne, I really do love you," Joe said, and pulled her T-shirt over the top of her head. "Do you think I could make love to you the way I do if I didn't love you?"

"I—I didn't know," Lynne admitted. She unbuttoned Joe's shirt and pushed it off his shoulders, baring his upper body to the moonlight. "You're so beautiful," she said, stroking his shoulders. She lowered her head for a minute before raising tear-filled eyes to Joe. "I can't believe you love me," she admitted, her face wreathed in a smile. "I was afraid it would never happen."

"And why were you afraid of that?" Joe asked softly. He leaned forward and captured her lips in a long, slow kiss. "You'd better believe it, woman," he said as he pushed her bra from her shoulders. "I love you, Lynne."

"I love you, too, Joe." She wound her arms around his neck. "Or could you already tell?"

"I could hope," Joe admitted. Lynne pulled him close; they met in another searing embrace, their bodies warm with desire. Lynne moaned and arched to him as Joe pulled her closer. "Oh, Lynne, I love you so much," he said. He pushed her gently onto the quilt, raining hot, fiery kisses down her face and her neck.

Lynne's face, staring up into Joe's, was a study in happiness. "You don't know how I've longed to hear that," she admitted. Her fingers explored his handsome face.

Joe continued kissing her shoulders and her breasts, bathing first one nipple and then the other with the sweet torment of his tongue. Lynne twisted her head from side to side, savoring the sweetness of his tender touch. When her breasts were ripe with longing, Joe's tender lips moved lower on her body, kissing their way down her midriff until they reached the barrier of her jeans.

Joe unzipped the jeans and pulled them down, careful not to lose her panties in the dark. "Wouldn't want anybody to find them in the next few days," he said, and put them in his pocket. "Although, as flimsy as they are, I don't know why you bother."

"So a certain sexy cowboy can take them off," Lynne said as she unzipped Joe's pants. At last they were both nude, the light from the moon turning them into silver statues.

Joe framed Lynne's face in his hands. "You're a beautiful woman," he whispered, and kissed the lips that were opening to protest. "Yes, you are, you're beautiful to me."

Lynne almost cried with happiness. "Thank you," she whispered. Joe continued where he had left off a few minutes ago, stroking and caressing her waist and soft stomach with his lips and his tongue. He touched her there until she was moaning with pleasure. So caught up was she in their storm of passion, she was hardly aware that he had moved even lower, and it was only when his tongue had made the first tentative foray that she realized what was happening.

"Relax, Lynne, and let me give you something more," Joe said, and he worked absolute magic on her body. His lips caressed her intimately, and Lynne let herself go amid the storm of pleasure he was arousing in her. She moaned, her head thrashing back and forth on the pillow, as Joe brought her nearer and nearer a shattering climax, and Lynne gasped, feeling the first powerful explosion tear through her body. One after another, spasms of delight shook her, leaving her weak and spent when the storm was over.

Joe moved over her. "I can't wait any longer," he confessed as he joined his body to hers. Lynne gripped the hard muscles of his waist, the strength of his possession rekindling the fire within her, and pulled him toward her as he thrust deep into her sweetness. Lynne moved with Joe, arching herself to him so as to bring them more closely together, moaning as the passion built within her so that she was on fire for him. They rocked together, giving and taking and sharing what they both now knew was love. When Joe felt her stiffen beneath him, he gave himself up to the powerful tremors of passionate release shaking his body.

Joe rested his head on Lynne's shoulder. "I don't know about you, but I just died and went to heaven."

Lynne smiled sleepily into the darkness. "Me too. Twice, even," she said, and kissed him. "I wouldn't have believed it before, but it's so much better now that I know you love me." She propped her head on her elbow. "You do love me romantically, don't you, Joe?"

"Yes, I love you romantically, Lynne. Is there any other way to love you?"

"I guess not." She placed a gentle kiss on his eyelid.

Joe sat up and pulled her to a sitting position beside him. "I have something I want to ask you," he said, holding her hand.

Lynne's heart leaped to her throat at the loving expression and the hesitancy on Joe's face. "Ask," she commanded him.

"Will you be my wife?" he said quietly.

"Yes, Joe, I would be proud to be your wife," she answered, her eyes shimmering with tears of joy.

Joe kissed one lone tear that escaped to her cheek. "That's part of why I brought you to see the graves," he said. "Those were the first Stocktons to ranch on this land. They were married for over sixty years. I want us to be like them."

"So do I," Lynne whispered. Joe kissed her again, and the two of them curled up together on the blanket and stared up at the stars.

"We can start making some plans tomorrow. Tonight I just want to hold you."

Lynne nodded. She had never dreamed she could be so happy. Joe had told her that he loved her, and that he wanted to marry her and live with her for the rest of his life. And he had said he found her beautiful. Maybe Laura had been right after all—maybe she was too sensitive about her looks. Joe had fallen in love with her in spite of her outward appearance. He loved her deeply and passionately, as a man loves a woman. At least that was the way Lynne hoped he loved her. Surely he wouldn't ask her to marry him for any other reason!

Joe cradled Lynne close to him as a soft wind caressed their bodies. It seemed like a miracle. Lynne had agreed to marry him, and had cried because she was so happy. Joe blinked back happy tears of his own. The diabetes had not sent her packing. Of course, he had not brought up the subject, even though he probably should have. But

147

he hated to spoil such a romantic moment by reminding
her of what she would have to deal with as the wife of a
diabetic. She already knew, and besides, he hadn't really
wanted to find out if she had any reservations about him.

CHAPTER EIGHT

Joe and Lynne sat in Laura's living room holding hands, their faces wreathed in smiles. "We wanted you to be almost the first to know," Lynne said happily. "Joe and I are getting married."

"You are? When?" Laura demanded.

"As soon as we can get a wedding arranged," Joe said.

"Hey, that's wonderful," Tony said. He leaned over and shook Joe's hand.

Laura threw her arms around Lynne's neck. "You said we were almost the first to know," she said. "Did you call mother this morning?"

"Yes, and she sounded both relieved and excited. I think she had figured out what was going on. And Joe called his mother today after I left."

"Was she excited?" Laura asked.

"So excited she's coming down tomorrow to bring Lynne the traditional family engagement ring," Joe said. "It was my grandmother Stockton's, and Mom is so thrilled that one of us is finally getting married that she can hardly wait to get it on Lynne's finger!"

"That's sweet of your mother," Lynne said.

Joe shook his head. "My mother may be many fine things, but sweet isn't one of them," he said. "Actually,

149

she's known around Dallas as the Tiny Tornado. If Lynne and I want to make any of our plans ourselves, we'll have to do it between now and tomorrow, when Mom gets here." He smiled and pulled out a piece of paper. "Here's some ideas Lynne and I worked out last night in b—uh, I mean, last night." He turned red and Laura giggled. "We'd like to have the two of you stand up for us, and Laurina could be our flower girl."

Laura leaned forward and poured Joe another glass of tea. "I'd love to stand with Lynne, but don't you have a friend from Dallas you'd like to have with you? How about your old roommate?"

Joe shook his head quickly, remembering how Sharon Kovaks had hurt Lynne. "No, I'd rather have Tony, since he'll be family."

Tony nodded his agreement.

"And we want to get married on the ranch, under the tree in front of the house, if the weather permits," Joe continued. "Informal reception—we'll let Mom plan that so she won't feel too left out."

"Honeymoon?" Laura asked.

Joe and Lynne looked at each other and laughed. "Fishing, what else? Probably down the coast of Mexico," Lynne volunteered. "Of course, we can't leave the ranch for too long."

"Big wedding?" Laura asked.

" 'Fraid so," Joe admitted. "All the relatives on both sides come to nearly fifty, and all of Lynne's fellow officers will want to come, and I'm inviting some of my friends from Dallas. We can count on a crowd."

Joe and Lynne spent over an hour with Tony and Laura, talking about the wedding and other things. Lynne's eyes sparkled, and Tony and Laura thought privately that she had never looked happier, or more attractive, in her life.

As they were rising to go, Tony pulled Joe aside to share a joke with him, leaving Lynne alone with Laura.

"You were right," Lynne said quietly, her face glowing. "He did fall in love with me, Laura, in spite of how I look."

"I told you that looks just don't matter that much," Laura said.

Lynne wrinkled her forehead. "I don't think I would go that far," she admitted. "They do matter sometimes. Joe just managed to rise above them."

Laura started to say something, but the men's whoops of laughter interrupted her. Joe laughed all the way to the car, and was still wiping the tears out of his eyes when they had reached the highway. Lynne, who loved a good joke, begged Joe to let her in on the secret. At first Joe refused, but Lynne persisted until he finally gave in, and he laughed even harder when she didn't get the punch line.

Joe was still amused when he pulled up in front of Lynne's apartment. "I can't believe you didn't get it."

"Sorry, I've led a sheltered life."

Joe pulled her close for a long, tender kiss. "Can't say that I mind," he admitted. "Would you like to come out after work and meet Mom? She's driving down from San Antonio tomorrow morning, and should be here by the time you get off work. I'll cook you both supper."

"I'd like that," Lynne said, although she felt uneasy about meeting Joe's mother. Reva Stockton was the wife of a prominent Dallas attorney, and if Joe's looks were anything to go by, she was probably beautiful. Lynne took a deep breath and reminded herself that Joe loved

151

her and that he wanted to marry her. If Reva didn't like her, tough. But she hoped that Reva would like her, as her family liked Joe. "About what time?" she asked.

"The usual," Joe said, kissing her cheek. "I hate to be a spoilsport, but isn't that your telephone?"

"I bet it's mother." She ran up the stairs and answered the telephone on the fifth ring. "Hello, mother? Oh, it's you, Ben. What's up?" Lynne listened for two minutes and had just hung up when Joe wandered inside. "Gee, thanks," she said, glowering at him.

"What did I do?" Joe asked, bewildered.

"That was Ben. He wants me to go in and track aliens for half the night with Bert." She pulled off her sundress and got into a uniform.

"So what did I have to do with that?" Joe demanded.

"You heard the telephone!" Lynne stuck out her tongue at him. Then she pulled on her boots and strapped on her Sam Brown. "Oh, well, I can hardly wait to tell them the news!"

"Have a fun night," Joe said wickedly. They left her apartment together, and later Joe dreamed of Lynne while Lynne tracked aliens all night long.

Lynne tapped on the door of Joe's house, peeking inside. "Joe, I'm here." It seemed strange to knock, but Reva Stockton's Cadillac was parked in front, and she didn't want to seem too familiar.

Joe poked his head around the kitchen door. "Come on in, hon," he said. "Mom's just getting dressed. She'll be out in a minute."

Lynne joined Joe in the kitchen. "She brought the ring with her," he said as he mixed the salad. "I hope you don't mind wearing it."

"I'll be proud to wear it," Lynne assured him. Joe pointed to the tea pitcher and Lynne started taking out glasses.

"It's a beauty," Joe commented. "Nicer than anything I could afford to get you right now. Say, will you get me the platter out of the top cabinet? Mom wants to use it for her chicken."

Lynne stretched her long arms over the top of the refrigerator and was just removing the platter when she heard a voice behind her.

"Joe, have you gotten the platter down yet? I want to have everything nice for Lynne when she gets here."

Lynne turned around and stared down at Reva Stockton. Barely five feet tall, Reva was still as slim as a girl, and her classically molded, finely sculptured face could have belonged to a model. Not one of Reva's artfully arranged gray hairs was out of place, and the tiny woman was dressed in a pair of chic white slacks and a silk top. Lynne swallowed as she handed Reva the platter. "Hello, Mrs. Stockton, I'm Lynne Kosler."

"Mom, this is Lynne," Joe stood beside Lynne and put his arm around her waist. "Lynne, my mother."

Reva tried, but she couldn't hide her astonishment. She looked from Joe to Lynne, and quickly hid her feelings behind a bright smile while extending her hand to Lynne. "Hello, Lynne. Welcome to the family."

"Thank you, Mrs. Stockton," Lynne murmured, engulfing Reva's hand in her own.

"Please, make it Reva. And thank you for the platter. None of us is quite tall enough to reach it."

"No problem," Lynne said. Joe blushed and Lynne knew that he felt embarrassed by the difference in their heights. "Did you have a nice drive down?"

"Yes, I did," Reva said, moving to the stove. Her motions quick and efficient, she basted the baking chicken and checked her vegetables. "But I was tired of sitting behind the wheel and doing nothing. I insisted that Joe let me cook supper."

"It smells delicious," Lynne said sincerely, quickly revising her image of Reva as a pampered woman who let the maid do all her cleaning and cooking. The three of them worked together to prepare supper, and somehow, Reva managed to cook the chicken and the vegetables and not get a spot on her flawlessly white pants, or chip her perfect manicure. Lynne's old feelings of inadequacy crept over her again, as they had the night of Joe's party. She tried to convince herself that Reva Stockton would intimidate any future daughter-in-law, but admitted that Reva's first reaction to her had been disappointment.

Determined not to let her own feelings or Reva's reaction get to her, Lynne contributed her part to the conversation at dinner. She shared some of her more exciting INS exploits with Reva, who seemed genuinely interested in Lynne's unusual occupation. Lynne in turn learned that Reva kept her own five-bedroom house, served on the steering committees of three large charity organizations, and in her spare time liked to fish as much as she and Joe did. Joe sat back and let the two women he loved most in the world get to know each other better. He could tell that his mother had been taken aback by Lynne at first, but he had never known Reva to be anything but fair. Once she got to know Lynne, she would love her. He knew that Lynne was a little intimidated, but who wouldn't be? His mother even intimidated him sometimes.

As Joe had predicted, Reva launched in and offered

her help with the wedding. She seemed a little disappointed in their wish to have it at the ranch, saying that she loved church weddings, but when Lynne and Joe insisted, she offered to arrange the reception herself. Lynne said that she'd be delighted to have the help and earned a wink and a smile from Joe.

They finished dinner and the three of them loaded the dishwasher. Joe insisted on showing off Marshmallow, and Lynne, who was getting a little anxious to see her engagement ring, trotted impatiently down to the barn with them. Reva cooed over the little colt and asked several questions about the ranch before she and Lynne returned to the house, leaving Joe to perform a forgotten chore. Reva caught the excited look on Lynne's face. "I guess you're dying to see the ring," Reva said. "I'd get it now, but I promised Joe I would let him give it to you."

"I know it's silly, but, yes, I'm very excited," Lynne admitted. "I've dreamed of having an engagement ring all my life."

Reva looked down at Lynne's large, bony hand and bit her lip. "We'll probably have to get it sized," she said.

Lynne looked at Reva's small, thin hands and laughed. "I would have been surprised if we hadn't. I just want to see the ring."

Joe came in, and he and his mother disappeared into the guest bedroom, returning a moment later with a satin jewelry box. "Here it is," Joe said. He took the ring out of the box. "Let's see how it looks."

Lynne held out her hand and Joe slid the tiny filigreed ring down her finger, pushing a little to get it over her top knuckle. Lynne stared down at the small, exquisitely fashioned ring and fought back tears. It was beautiful, with an ice-white diamond in the center of a web of spun

155

gold, but there was no way she could wear it. In order to expand it enough for Lynne to get it on her large finger, the delicate filigree work on the sides would have to be destroyed. "It doesn't fit, Joe," she whispered. "It's so beautiful, but I can't wear it."

Joe looked down, frowning. "Lynne, I'm sorry. Maybe if we took it to a jeweler?"

Reva picked up Lynne's hand and stared at the delicate ring. "Maybe it could be altered, but I'm afraid it would ruin the filigree. Besides, Joe, it really doesn't look right on her finger. She needs a big, bold ring. You know, the kind I can't wear," she added ruefully.

Joe handed the ring back to his mother. "I'll save it for your daughter," Reva told Lynne softly. "Lynne, maybe he can find you something in Houston. They have some elegant things there."

Joe winced. "I hope they have a good installment plan."

"You don't have to buy me a diamond," Lynne told him quietly, her dream of having a beautiful ring crumbling before her eyes. "I can wear a band." She hoped that Joe would insist on buying her one anyway.

To her disappointment Joe looked almost relieved. "Well, if you're sure, it would take a burden off me," he said honestly. "A solitaire these days costs a small fortune."

"I'm sure, Joe," Lynne lied, hiding her hurt behind eyes that had become shuttered again.

Lynne carried two diet soft drinks into the living room. "Reva, are you sure I can't get you anything?" she asked on handing one of the Cokes to Joe. The hot afternoon

156

sun beat through the windows, but it seemed cool inside compared with the heat outside.

"No, Lynne, I'm fine. I had just finished some iced tea when you two came in. Where had your runaway gotten out?"

Lynne had come out for a visit and found Joe trying to round up a stubborn old cow who had somehow managed to get out on the road. Lynne and Joe now were both hot and sweaty, a grimy contrast to Reva's constant freshness.

"Over near the west gate," Joe said. "Some of the wire was down. Lynne nailed it back up for me, but she scratched herself in the process."

Reva turned Lynne's arm over and made a face at the long, jagged gash. "It's not deep, but you'd better let me take care of it for you," Reva said, motioning for Lynne to follow her to the bathroom. Reva sat Lynne down on the toilet and sponged the dirt out of the cut. "I know I sound like a mother hen, but I don't want you getting an infection before the wedding." She stood blotting away the water with a clean towel. "It isn't all that far away."

"I know," Lynne said. Joe had insisted that they get married on the second Saturday in September. "Joe sure didn't give us much time. Everybody in town's going to think we had to get married!"

Reva laughed charmingly and winked. "Just be careful between now and then," she said, laughing harder when Lynne blushed. "Have you and your sister got your dresses picked out?"

"Maria's making them," Lynne replied. "She makes all my clothes. I'm too tall to buy much in the stores."

"I'm sure your dress will be lovely," Reva said. She thought a minute. "I was surprised that Joe didn't ask

Les Kovaks to be his best man. They've always been so close."

"I think it's because of me," Lynne said quietly. "Sharon made some unkind remarks about my—uh, me, and Joe knew that they'd hurt my feelings."

Reva's eyes narrowed on Lynne's pensive face. "That's all right. I never particularly liked the woman, anyway. She can be a real cat."

"I've noticed," Lynne said.

Reva got out the antiseptic and put some on a cotton ball. "Yes, and she carries on like she's the belle of Dallas or something," Reva said offhandedly. "The truth of it is, she's nothing to look at without all that makeup she wears, because I saw her once at the salon without it. It's amazing what the right cosmetics will do." She carefully doctored the cut on Lynne's arm and inspected it. "Do you think you need a bandage? It will probably heal better if you leave it open."

"No, I'm fine," Lynne said. Lynne discreetly studied Reva's face while Reva recapped the ointment. Was Reva's face less than perfect underneath all the makeup she wore?

Later, as she drove home, Lynne thought about Reva's comment regarding Sharon Kovaks. Reva had not just been gossiping about Sharon—she had been hinting, once again, that Lynne ought to fix herself up a little more. In the week and a half since Reva had arrived, she had dropped several hints that Lynne should be more aware of her hairstyle and her makeup. Lynne resented Reva's little suggestions, yet she was beginning to wonder if she had a point. She found herself remembering the way all of Joe's women friends had looked the night of the party.

Surely they weren't all the raving beauties she had perceived them to be that evening!

Later, after she had showered, Lynne carefully inspected her image in the mirror. Would a professional makeup job make a difference in the way she looked? Sure, she always wore makeup, but she had never learned to apply it the way the models in the magazines did. She ran her fingers through her hair and fluffed it around her face. And her hair—what would a different stylist say about her hairstyle? Would she look better if she changed it?

Lynne sat down on the side of her bed and riffled through the Sunday paper for an ad she remembered having seen. A New York stylist was supposed to be at one of the shopping malls for a couple of days this week doing makeovers. Lynne ripped the ad from the paper and shoved it into her wallet. She would make an appointment tomorrow and go to the stylist. She knew better than to think she would come out of it looking like Reva, or even Sharon Kovaks, but it might help her. It was worth a try.

Lynne took off her uniform shirt and wrapped a belted smock around herself, reveling in the unaccustomed feeling of being pampered. She was paying a bundle for this, so she might as well enjoy it! Luckily, she had been called out in the middle of the night to help with a tracking, and was now free for the rest of the day to let Henri, the stylist from the Big Apple, work his magic on her. A young girl washed Lynne's hair and wrapped it in a warm towel, and when Henri motioned her over a few minutes later, she sat down in his chair almost eagerly.

The last girl who had left his chair had looked fabulous, and Lynne fervently hoped she would too.

Henri turned Lynne so that he could look into her face. Carefully he scrutinized her, feature by feature, studying her hazel eyes, her long nose, her narrow lips. "You will never be beautiful, but you have the potential for being a striking woman," he said. "And let me tell you, striking's much better than pretty in the long run. Much less boring."

"You don't have to convince me, I'll gladly settle for striking." Lynne grinned.

Henri grinned back. "Well, let's get on with it." He unwrapped her hair and combed it down around her face and shoulders. "I bet you wear this parted in the middle and flat to your head," he said disapprovingly. "With your narrow face and your figure, you need volume on the sides." He held Lynne's hair up around her face. "See? You need a perm to put some body in that hair. That's first on the agenda."

Lynne started to protest, but refrained. She was paying this man for his advice, and she was going to follow it. She sat patiently while Henri cut and then rolled her hair, applying the smelly perming solution over the rollers. She was alternately neutralized, unrolled, shampooed, and rinsed, and an hour later she stared at her hair in the mirror as Henri held out section after section to be gently blown and styled. "See how much more body your hair has now with the perm?" Henri asked.

Lynne watched it fall into an artful tangle of curls around her head and down her shoulders. "Yes, I can tell the difference," she murmured as Henri used the curling iron on a stubborn lock. Her hair was different, all right, but she wasn't sure she really liked it.

"Now, if you'll wear it in a side part, it will draw attention away from your nose," Henri suggested, swiftly combing in a left part.

When Henri had her hair arranged to his idea of perfection, he turned to Lynne's face. "You need to play up your eyes." He opened his makeup palette and picked up a disposable brush. "They're your best feature, and we're going to be sure they're fabulous."

Lynne had never thought of her eyes as beautiful, but Henri must know what he was doing. He worked on her slowly, explaining each step and writing down the product on a face chart, but by the time he was half finished with her eyes, Lynne was hopelessly lost. Making her face like this would be like painting a color-by-number kit every morning before work!

Unaware of her confusion, Henri continued making Lynne up, adding a dab of this here, and that there, for the better part of an hour. He showed her how to minimize the circles under her eyes, to draw her cheekbones upward with properly applied blush, to shorten the length of her face with concealer, to widen her narrow lips with a lip pencil. Lynne's disappointment grew keener by the minute with the realization that the hoped-for transformation was not going to happen. Henri's cosmetics subtracted as much as they added. Before, her face had been long and narrow, but now it was obviously shaded. Her thin lips were now wider, but they were garishly bright, and the thick base and blusher added years to her appearance.

Finally, when Lynne thought she could stand no more of his plucking and dabbing, Henri stepped back and handed her a mirror. "What did I tell you?" he asked as she stared into her now unfamiliar face. "Didn't I tell you I would make you striking?"

Well, that was one way to put it. Lynne felt as if she had been painted up for Halloween, but she said nothing of what she really felt, and thanked Henri for his hard work. Henri bubbled on a little about how wonderful she now looked, and he reminded her that his fee was redeemable in purchases from his company's line.

Sick with disappointment, Lynne left the store and got into her car, where she stared into the rearview mirror for several minutes. She might grow to like the permanent, but the rest of the afternoon had been a waste. Even a professional makeup artist couldn't do much with her! She wanted to go home and wash the makeup off, but she couldn't. She was due out at Joe's within the hour. Besides, maybe she was wrong. Joe and Reva might think the new Lynne was just great!

Lynne parked her car under the shade tree in the front yard and walked around to the back, since she wanted to pay Marshmallow a visit before going into the house. She had just passed the open kitchen window when she froze, hearing Reva's voice and her name mentioned. She started to hurry on, but heard Joe laughing at something Reva was saying.

"Now, stop your laughing and listen to me, Joe," Reva said firmly. "I'm trying to talk about your future with that girl, and all you can do is laugh in my face."

"I'm not laughing, mom, honest," Joe said. Lynne could hear the amusement in his voice. "I'm listening to you."

"Thank you," Reva said with dignity. "Joe, I have nothing against Lynne, she seems to be a nice enough girl, but are you sure you want to marry her? You've

162

always dated such cute girls before, and she's so plain. Are you sure she's the one for you, Joe?"

Lynne held her breath, waiting for Joe to tell Reva that he was in love with her, and that was why he was marrying her, and he didn't care that she wasn't beautiful.

To her amazement Joe started to laugh again. "So what if she's plain, Mom? It really doesn't matter what my ranch hand or my fishing buddy looks like, does it?"

Lynne felt anger and hurt burn through her. He had lied to her—he didn't love her, not the way a man loves a woman. He just wanted a workhorse to help him run his ranch. And she was a pretty good nurse when he had an insulin overdose. Fury rose up within her as the tears welled in her eyes. Angrily, she wiped them away and marched into Joe's kitchen.

"Lynne, honey, you're early," Joe said, standing up. "What have you done to your hair?"

"Save it, Joe," Lynne snapped. "I'm not staying. It's all off. I wouldn't marry you if you were the last man on the face of this earth!" She turned on her heel and left the room, slamming the back door and running toward her car.

Joe and Reva stared at one another in astonishment. "She heard you, Joe," Reva said.

Joe ran out the front door, catching up with Lynne just as she reached her car. "No, Lynne, honey, I can explain," he pleaded, blocking her way to the car.

"You've already explained everything to your mother just beautifully," Lynne said bitingly, the trembling of her lower lip giving away her hurt. "You don't love me."

"Lynne, yes, I—"

"All you want is a ranch hand out here!" Lynne yelled down into his upturned face. "You want someone to clean your fish and deliver your calves and nurse you when your diabetes is acting up! Well, you can count me out, Joe! I want to be loved."

Joe stepped back as though she had slapped him. "You think I don't love you. You think that's all I want," he said, his face white with anger. "You think I just want a nurse for when I'm sick."

"Well, don't you?" Lynne demanded. "You don't even love me enough to buy me a pretty ring, Joe." She sniffed back fresh tears. "I always wanted one, you know." She wiped her eyes, streaking mascara across her cheek. "I wanted to be loved, Joe. I wanted you to love me romantically, the way a man's supposed to love a woman."

"And you don't think I do that," Joe said flatly, his anger evident in his trembling voice. "You think all I want is a nurse when the diabetes is acting up. *Damn* you for that, Lynne."

"I heard what you said, Joe. You couldn't have made yourself much clearer." She swallowed the lump in her throat. "Let me go home, Joe," she said wearily. She got into her car and left the ranch, leaving a cloud of dust behind her.

Joe stood rooted to the spot as he watched Lynne drive away. She had been hurt by what she thought she had heard, and he ought to go after her, but the crack about the diabetes had made him angry, and it had hurt. He couldn't help it if he got sick sometimes! Cursing under his breath, he went into the house and slammed the door behind him. He would talk to Lynne later, after they had both calmed down.

Lynne watched closely in the rearview mirror until she saw Joe go into the house. So he wasn't going to follow her. That meant she must have been right. He didn't love her as she wanted to be loved. She hadn't been able to inspire the kind of feelings in Joe that she so wanted him to feel. To him she was just a live-in ranch hand.

Lynne gave up trying to fight the tears and let them run freely down her cheeks. She had been right all along —she simply didn't have what it took to inspire the love of a man like Joe. He was willing to marry her for what she could do on his ranch, but for him love didn't enter the picture. Damn him for having lied to her, for having let her think he loved her! Lynne wiped her cheeks, but she couldn't stem the flow of tears. She wasn't sure what hurt most—the fact that Joe had lied to her, or that she didn't have what it took to inspire his love. Either one alone would have been bad enough, but the two together were almost more than she could bear.

CHAPTER NINE

Lynne entered her apartment and marched straight to the bathroom. She scrubbed off all the cosmetics and watched the makeup-stained suds drip down into the sink, washing down the drain along with Lynne's dreams of a future with Joe. She raised her head and stared at herself. Her eyes were red from crying, but her clear, young skin could be seen once more.

Lynne hated the sight of herself at that moment. She took a long, hot shower and tried to eat supper, a part of her hoping that Joe would knock on her door. But if he came, nothing he could say would make her feel any better about what he had told Reva. She had thought he loved her, in spite of her plain appearance, but he didn't. That was clear now.

Lynne got herself a beer and carried it out to the pool. She drank it slowly, watching a bikinied teenage girl play water volleyball with a couple of boys while her plump friend sat on the sidelines looking miserable. Lynne's heart went out to the fat girl—she knew all too well what it was like to be on the outside looking at the pretty girls having fun. Hadn't she been doing that all her life?

The young people finished their volleyball game and the four of them wandered off, both of the boys showering the pretty girl with attention while the fat one just tagged along. It just wasn't fair! Why couldn't men see past a pretty face to the woman who was inside? Lynne remembered the night when Joe first made love to her, the night he had told her that she was a lovely woman. Had he been lying to her? Was he just telling her what he thought she wanted to hear? He had sounded so sincere that night, about her looks not mattering to him. And they wouldn't, Lynne thought sadly, if all he cared about was her talent on the ranch. Joe was right—ranch hands *don't* have to be pretty.

Lynne sat by herself in the poolside chair, letting dusk fall around her as the sun went down and the sky darkened from blue to purple to black. She stared at the reflections of the porch lights in the water, examining her feelings about Joe. Even though he had hurt her, she did still love him. A part of her would still like to spend the rest of her life with him, but could she do it knowing that he didn't love her? It would be hard, but she could make herself forget what she had overheard this afternoon. She could forgive Joe and go ahead with the wedding, and pretend he loved her the way she loved him. She could live on his ranch, help him take care of his cattle and horses, and eventually have his children, and probably be reasonably content doing so.

But if she did that, she would miss out on the one thing in life that she wanted most. The reflections in the pool water shimmered as Lynne's eyes filled with tears. Joe didn't love her. Oh, he liked her well enough, and he admired her, but the deep, romantic love she felt was absent on Joe's part. She was his ranch hand and his fishing buddy, but she wasn't the love of his life. If she did marry him, knowing he didn't love her, she would spend the rest of her life terrified that he would someday meet a beautiful, passionate woman who would be the very special one for him.

Lynne returned to her apartment. She started to call Laura and pour out her heart, but changed her mind. It was late, and if she called, Laura would be over here tonight, and Lynne wasn't up to talking about it yet. Besides, maybe Joe would come over tomorrow or the next day and they would talk.

But Joe didn't call Lynne or come by to see her—not that day, or the next, or the one after that. Lynne had hoped Joe would at least try to talk to her and explain, but her hope was dying as the fourth day came and went with no word from him. She had been right—Joe didn't love her, and he didn't even care enough to call her and formally call off their engagement. Lynne said nothing at work, hoping that her misery didn't show on the outside. She volunteered to work a couple of night patrols simply to keep from lying awake until all hours, staring at the ceiling and wishing Joe would call.

Lynne could feel herself growing tense and irritable, so after work she put in an extra-long session at the exercise club. As she pulled up to her apartment, she saw Laura's car and her very pregnant sister waiting for her on the front step. "I called the ranch looking for you and the foreman said Joe and his mother had left town, so I took a chance that you might want supper"—and she waved a delicious-smelling bag under Lynne's nose. "Tony and Laurina went to the zoo, but I didn't feel like traipsing around in the heat."

"So you sat around in the heat waiting for me." Lynne hugged her sister. "Come on in and I'll get us something to drink."

Lynne made iced tea while Laura set the table and unwrapped the hamburgers. Lynne wondered if Joe had gone with Reva back to Dallas, and how he had managed to get away from the ranch, as busy as he had been. She was sure of one thing—if he got behind again, he could find somebody else to help him out!

Laura sat down across from Lynne. "How are the wedding plans coming?" she asked, taking a bite of her hamburger. "I had expected to hear from you before now. That's why I called the ranch."

Lynne put her hamburger down. "The wedding's off," she said in a low voice.

"What?" Laura demanded, choking a little. "What happened? No, don't tell me right now. You look like you've lost weight since the last time I saw you, and when you're upset you don't eat. Eat now, and you can tell me later."

Laura immediately launched into a funny story about Laurina's nursery school. Grateful for Laura, Lynne gagged down most of the hamburger and about half the french fries while Laura chattered on about this and that. Laura frowned disapprovingly at Lynne's plate, so Lynne obligingly ate two more bites of the hamburger. She knew she hadn't lost any weight, but her emotional strain and fatigue had combined to make her face appear tired and pinched. She knew Laura was going to be upset about the breakup and didn't want her sister any more disturbed than she had to be.

Laura made them each a cup of decaffeinated coffee and Lynne sat down on the carpeted floor, stretching her legs out in front of her. "I hope you haven't bought the material for your dress," Lynne said sadly. "It's all off, Laura."

"What happened?" Laura asked. "You were both so happy! Didn't his mother like you?"

Lynne shrugged. "I don't know whether she liked me or not," she admitted. "I just know that she was horrified the first time she laid eyes on me."

"Why was she horrified?" Laura asked.

"Why do you think?" Lynne asked dryly. "She's five feet tall and about as beautiful as they come."

"But at least she didn't try to come between you and Joe," Laura said musingly. "Somehow, I don't think she could if she tried. Joe doesn't impress me as being a mama's boy."

"He isn't," Lynne agreed.

"So what happened? Did you and Joe have a fight?"

"Oh, Laura it was awful!" Lynne cried. "First I couldn't wear the family ring because my hands are too big, and Joe doesn't want to buy me one. Then Reva kept dropping these hints that I ought to fix myself up more and do my hair, so I went in to that makeover session at the shopping mall. It was horrible. I looked terrible when he was through, but I thought Joe and his mother might like me better that way. Anyway I went out to the ranch and overheard Reva ask Joe if he really wanted to marry a plain woman like me."

"And you turned tail and ran before you heard what he said," Laura said disapprovingly.

"I wish I had," Lynne said bitterly. "I might have been spared hearing him say that it doesn't matter what his ranch hand or his fishing buddy looks like!"

Laura sat a minute. "He really said that?" she asked quietly.

Lynne nodded. "I heard him clearly."

"So what did you do? Sneak off?"

"What do you think I am, Laura, a coward? I informed him that he was the last man on earth I would marry, and that I wasn't going to deliver his calves and nurse him when he was sick." Lynne stopped and wiped her eyes. "He doesn't love me, Laura. He just wants all the things I can do for him."

Laura sat for a minute. "And did you come to this conclusion after you had talked, or did you decide that Joe doesn't love you on the basis of one overheard remark?"

"What more could he say?" Lynne asked, anguish shadowing her eyes. "He doesn't love me—he sees me as a buddy to ranch and fish with. I should have known I didn't have what it took to make him fall in love with me." She raised her tear-filled eyes to Laura. "Why couldn't he have loved me, Laura? Why couldn't I have been born pretty enough to inspire him to love me the way Tony loves you?"

"Oh, Lynne, it isn't like that at all," Laura said compassionately.

"Isn't it?" Lynne asked bitterly. "It sure seems like it is. You pretty women have it made when it comes to men falling in love with you, while the rest of us get left out in the cold."

Laura raised her eyebrow and looked into Lynne's face. "When are you going to stop blaming your looks for everything that goes wrong with your lovelife?" she asked dryly.

Lynne stared up at Laura in shock. "W-what?"

"You heard me," Laura said tartly. "The minute anything goes wrong, you run to the mirror and blame it on your face. Lynne, that's ridiculous."

171

"It is not ridiculous!" Lynne said hotly. "Look at you. You're pretty, and Tony loves you, doesn't he?"

"For crying out loud, Lynne, I'm no raving beauty, and even if I were, I sure hope Tony loves me for something more than what I look like," Laura replied.

"But that's what attracted him in the first place," Lynne argued.

"Sure it was," Laura scoffed. "Stop and think, Lynne. How did Tony meet me?"

"You were in the infirmary and he was working there," Lynne recalled slowly.

"Yes, I was in the infirmary because I was covered with chicken pox," Laura said. "For the first two weeks Tony knew me, all he saw were pockmarks and Calomine lotion. He spent hours playing cards with me so I wouldn't scratch."

"But later—"

"There wasn't a later," Laura said. "Tony proposed before I ever checked out of there. We just didn't tell anyone for several months. He had never even seen me in a dress or makeup before he asked me to marry him."

"I didn't know that," Lynne said quietly.

"Look, I know you've always thought that the pretty girls have it made, but it isn't so. I'm reasonably attractive, I guess, but the only thing it ever got me was a few dates in high school and college, and some of them I could have done without. Nothing of what I have today —Tony, Laurina, my job—is due to my face or my figure."

Lynne chewed on her lower lip. "I wish I could believe you, Laura. But if that's true, why did he tell his mother a thing like that? Why didn't he tell her he loved me?"

"I don't know, Lynne. I don't know what Joe was

172

thinking when he said that, and I can't speak for him—maybe he really feels that way. But even if he does, there's another man out there who will love you. Beauty isn't what inspires a man's love, not in the long run. It's what you are on the inside that makes them keep loving you."

"That's what Joe said, and I believed him," Lynne observed, more to herself than to Laura.

"So believe him," Laura said firmly. "Believe both of us." She looked down into Lynne's face, seeing the unhappiness and the uncertainty. "The first thing you're going to have to do, Lynne, is to come to terms with the way you look. So you're not pretty. So what? You have your health, you have a good job, you have family—you have a lot more going for you than a lot of beautiful women. I bet there are any number of them who would trade places with you and not blink an eye."

"This is all well and good, but what about Joe?" Lynne asked.

"Talk to him again. Tell him what you heard and ask him what made him say it. You don't know, he might have meant something totally different from what you thought you heard."

"No, I don't want to do that," Lynne said quickly. "If he really cared about me, he could have said so that afternoon."

"Did you give him a chance, or did you fly off the handle?"

"I did most of the talking," Lynne admitted. "But he could have come after me, couldn't he? If he cared, he would have called or come by. It's been nearly a week."

"On the other hand, he may be waiting for you to make the first move," Laura said. "That crack about taking care of the diabetes was hitting below the belt, wasn't it? He can't help it when he gets sick."

"I don't want to talk to him," Lynne said stubbornly.

"Fine. Sit around miserable for the rest of your life," Laura said. "Lynne, *please* go talk to the man when he gets back to town," she pleaded. "You had such a good thing going with him. Don't blow it now."

"I'll think about it," Lynne said.

"That's the way to go," Laura said. She got up off the couch and hugged Lynne. "It will all work out, I promise you. Call me later in the week and let me know what you decide."

Lynne nodded and wished Laura a good-night. She found a movie on television, but her thoughts kept returning to what Laura had said. Laura insisted that beauty wasn't necessary to inspire a man's love, that what was on the inside counted. But Lynne simply couldn't bring herself to believe it, although she desperately wanted to. There was no way that Laura could convince her—only Joe could make her believe that her looks didn't matter.

Lynne got up and turned off the television set. She had to talk to Joe again. She had to find out what he really felt for her before she called the minister and canceled the wedding. She dreaded the thought of talking to Joe and having him confirm his lack of love for her, but she owed it to herself to find out how he felt.

Reluctantly, Lynne dialed Joe's number. The foreman answered and told her that Joe was expected to return sometime tomorrow afternoon. Lynne had to work tomorrow, but she would drive out after supper and talk with Joe. She dreaded the visit, but realized that it was necessary.

174

Her decision made, Lynne returned to the television movie and even managed to get a little interested. When it was over, she showered and washed her hair and dressed in an old nightgown. She cut herself a piece of cake and was just settling down on the couch when she heard a knock at the front door. "Who's there?" she asked quietly.

"Lynne, it's me. Joe. I know it's late, but can I come in?"

"Joe!" Lynne said, throwing open the door before she realized how she was dressed. Joe was wearing his city clothes and looked wonderful. "Uh, let me find something else to put on," she said as she turned to bolt.

Joe reached out and grabbed her wrist. "It's all right, Lynne."

"No, it's not."

Joe released her hand. "Don't take too long. I want to talk to you."

Since it was pointless to get back into her clothes, Lynne donned a pretty cotton gown and robe to match. Joe was sitting on the couch, his coat off and his tie loosened. "Can I get you anything to eat?" she asked.

"Just a piece of cheese or something. I stopped for dinner in Kingsville."

Lynne cut Joe a couple of slices of cheese and some apple wedges. "Have you been away on business?" she asked, handing Joe his plate and picking up the cake.

"You might say that," Joe said as he nibbled one of the pieces of cheese. He put it down and rubbed the back of his neck. "I'm tired," he admitted. "I'd forgotten how long that drive is from Dallas."

"You've driven all the way from Dallas?" Lynne demanded. "That's a twelve-hour trip!"

"Well, not quite that long in the Trans Am." Joe laughed. "Eat your cake. You look hungry."

Obediently Lynne ate her cake, her curiosity burning within her. What was Joe doing here tonight? Why had he come by to see her? Was he going to break off their relationship? She finished about half her cake and put the plate on the coffee table. Joe put his plate down beside hers and felt around in his coat pocket. "Come here, Lynne. I have something for you."

Lynne sat down on the couch beside Joe. He withdrew two jewelry boxes embossed with the name of a famous Dallas jeweler and handed her the larger of the two. Mystified, Lynne opened the box and gasped when she saw the wide gold band with a large cluster of diamonds gracing the center. "That's the closest I could come to a big solitaire, the kind Mom said would look right on your hand," Joe said quietly.

"Joe, it's beautiful." Lynne gasped, staring down into the shimmering diamonds. "But how—what? I thought you couldn't afford a ring!"

Joe shrugged and handed her the second box. Lynne's eyes widened even farther when she saw the diamond earrings, the clusters a smaller version of the one on her ring. "I thought they would look good with the ring," he said. "Do you like them, Lynne?"

"Of course I like them, Joe." She gazed down at the ring and the earrings with a troubled expression. "But how did you buy them? I thought you were broke."

"I am," Joe admitted. "I hope you don't mind staying with INS after we're married."

"No, I planned to make it a career," Lynne murmured.

"Anyway, I borrowed the money from Mom, and I'm going to be in hock to her for a while," Joe said frankly.

Lynne turned anguished eyes on Joe. "You didn't have to do that," she said. "Not if it was going to be a burden."

"Yes, I did," Joe said. "I never dreamed how much a fancy ring meant to you, Lynne, until the other day when you said I didn't care enough about you to buy one. I didn't realize how you felt or I would never have agreed to buy you a plain band." He took her hand in his and rubbed the back of it with his thumb. "Will this prove to you that I love you, Lynne? That I love you the way you want to be loved?"

Lynne pulled her hand away from Joe's and stood up, facing the window so he couldn't see the tears in her eyes or the trembling of her chin. "I don't know, Joe," she admitted. "It wasn't just the ring, you know. It was what I heard you tell your mother the other afternoon."

Joe closed both jewelry boxes and set them on the coffee table. "What exactly did you hear us say, Lynne?"

"Your mother asked you if you were sure you wanted to marry such a plain woman. I guess she can't help the way she feels, she's used to the pretty women you've dated in the past, but I thought you'd tell her that you loved me. You didn't do that, Joe." Lynne turned around and faced him, the tears in her eyes threatening to overflow. "You told her it didn't matter what a ranch hand or a fishing buddy looked like." Lynne stopped and sniffed. "Is that all I am to you, Joe? A ranch hand or a fishing buddy?"

Joe stared at Lynne gravely. "Do you really think, after the love we've shared, that's all you are to me?"

"I don't know," Lynne wailed miserably. "After you asked me to marry you, I thought you had fallen in love with me, that you loved me the way that I love you. And then you said a thing like that to your mother." Her eyes finally overflowed and she wiped them furiously.

Joe stood up and handed her his handkerchief. "Sit down, Lynne. We need to do some serious talking tonight, because I simply don't understand why you're so upset. You only heard half of what I told Mom. Your eavesdropping was late for the part when I said I loved you. The ranch-hand-and-fishing-buddy crack came later.

"And personally, I think they're all excellent reasons to marry you," Joe replied. "What I don't understand is why it upset you so much."

"Damn it, Joe, I don't *want* to be just a ranch hand or a fishing buddy! I want to be sure you love me, even if I'm not the most beautiful woman in the world!"

Joe stared at her for a moment. "So now we're getting somewhere. It's not just what I said about you, is it? You're still worried about your looks."

"Yes, I'm still worried about my looks," Lynne said quietly. "Joe, all my life I've been plain. It bothers me a lot, especially when I'm faced with the gorgeous women you used to go with or a beauty like your mother. She was horrified when she met me, Joe, as horrified as your friends were. It wouldn't be so bad if you weren't so handsome, but you are, and that just makes me look worse." She ran her fingers through her permed hair. "I tried, Joe. I even went in and got a makeover, but I just can't be beautiful."

"So what?" Joe asked softly.

"So what am I going to do when you get tired of looking at me?" Lynne replied. "What am I going to do when you get sick of your ranch hand and decide you want a prettier face on your pillow?"

"What am I going to do when you get tired of having to look down at your husband to talk to him?" Joe asked quietly. "Or when you get fed up with cooking for a diabetic, or serving dinner right on time, or nursing me through an insulin reaction?"

"Huh?" Lynne asked, confused.

Joe smiled at her sadly. "You think you're the only one who feels a little insecure? Lynne, you don't know the half of it. Mom may have looked at you a little strangely at first, but she spent the whole time she was here agonizing that you might change your mind about me because of the diabetes. I've lain awake at night, worrying that you might start thinking about what it will be like to be married to a diabetic, and change your mind about marrying me."

Lynne shook her head. "But the diabetes is no big deal," she protested.

"It's a lot bigger deal than your less-than-beautiful face," Joe said, stroking her cheek. "Look, Lynne, I'm sorry you don't come up to your own standards of perfection. But what you don't seem to understand is, that while you fall short of your own standards, *you don't fall short of mine.* I love you dearly, just the way you are." He caressed the waving hair at her temple. "I even like the new hairstyle."

Lynne touched her face lightly with her fingertips. "But I'm not beautiful."

"I don't care about that. That's what I was trying to tell mother. I didn't fall in love with you for your looks, or in spite of them. They just don't enter the picture. Think back over the last few months, Lynne. If the situation had been reversed and I had been homely, would it really have made any difference in our relationship?"

Lynne thought a minute and shook her head. "No, it really wouldn't have," she said thoughtfully.

"See what I mean? It wouldn't have mattered at all. Lynne, what you didn't hear me tell Mom was that it doesn't make any difference to me how you look—I fell in love with you for the person you are. You're a wonderful woman, Lynne, and we share so much. Please, Lynne, believe me when I tell you that I love you. I admit that I didn't fall in love with your face or your figure. I fell in love with you here"—he kissed the middle of her forehead—"and here." He placed his hand over her heart.

Lynne stared into Joe's eyes and saw the love shining back at her. "You do love me, don't you?" she breathed.

"Oh, dear God, Lynne, *yes!*" Joe crushed her to him and covered her lips in a deep, searching kiss. Lynne wrapped her arms around his neck, holding him tightly to her as happy tears rolled down her cheeks. Joe kissed her for a long moment, his hands caressing her wavy hair, his lips paying homage to the love they shared.

Lynne returned kiss for kiss, touch for touch, until a thought occurred to her and she pulled away from Joe, creating a little distance between them. Joe frowned at the serious expression on her face. "What's wrong?" he asked.

"Joe, I have no doubt that you love me. But what about your children? What if they look like me? How are you going to feel about a little girl if she's plain? I think Mother was always a little disappointed in me, and I wouldn't want you to feel that way about your child."

"How's our daughter going to feel about a daddy she towers over?" Joe asked teasingly, before his face sobered. "I'd love any child we had together, Lynne, and be proud of him or her. You ought to know that. But you're the one who ought to be worrying about your future offspring. Your children might not be the most beautiful in the world, but at least they'd be healthy. My children have a good chance of having diabetes. How would you feel about having a less-than-perfect child?"

"I'd hide the ice cream and carry on, Joe. I knew when you asked me to marry you that we'd face that possibility, and although it frightens me a little, if it does happen we'll cope. It doesn't put me off having children, if that's what you're worried about."

Joe shook his head. "And you don't understand why I love you," he said, capturing her lips in a long, lingering kiss. "Lynne, you have to be one of the most special people I've ever known." He reached over and picked up the jewelry boxes. "Lynne, will you marry this short diabetic?"

"Yes, Joe, this gawky, plain woman will marry you," Lynne said.

They both laughed, and Joe took the ring from the box and placed it on her finger. "Now comes the fun part," Joe said, and he pushed her hair behind her ear and kissed the delicate shell. With gentle fingers he removed her plain hoop earrings. One at a time he carefully placed the diamond clusters on her ears, ceremonially kissing each ear before and after he put the earring on. He ran to the bathroom and got her hand mirror. "Do you like them?" he asked eagerly.

Lynne turned her head this way and that, admiring the earrings, then held our her hand and looked at the ring. "They're beautiful," she said. "And the ring looks just perfect."

"Mom had to help me pick it out," Joe said. "Lynne, she really does like you," he assured her.

"I'm glad," Lynne admitted. She turned to Joe and threw her arms around his neck. "Joe, you've made me the happiest woman in the world."

Joe hugged her tightly. "Lynne, you've made me happier than I ever thought I could be." He held her face between his hands. "I never thought I'd find a woman with whom I could share so many of the things I love." He tipped her head and covered her lips with his, caressing the inside of her mouth with his tender tongue.

Lynne inched herself closer to him, stroking the hard muscles of his shoulders, savoring the sweetness of his kisses. They touched and clung together for a long time, reaffirming the love they had spoken of earlier. Both of them were panting and breathless when Joe finally raised his head. "I've missed you so much, Lynne," he said quietly, the depth of his emotion evident in the tension in his voice. "Please don't ever run away from me again."

"Never," Lynne promised, and she held Joe tightly to her. "I'll never doubt your love for me."

Joe planted a hard, sweet kiss on her lips. "I am invited to stay the night, aren't I?" he asked as he got up off the floor.

"Of course," Lynne assured him. "Tonight and every night for the rest of your life. Joe, where are you going?"

"Unless you want to start those little kids we talked about tonight, I'd better get my suitcase," Joe said, laughing when Lynne turned red. He returned a couple of minutes later to find Lynne turning back the bed. He kissed the back of her neck and caressed her waist. Shedding his tie, he said, "If you don't mind, I'd like to use your shower."

"Allow me." She pulled the tie from around his neck and tossed it across the chair. His shirt soon followed, and his pants and his socks. Lynne sat back on the bed and gazed at the hard-muscled perfection of Joe's body. "You're so beautiful," she said. The desire was growing within her.

Joe leaned down and kissed her lips. "So are you, and don't you ever forget it." He pushed the robe from her shoulders. "Come shower with me."

"I just had one," Lynne protested. "Look, my hair's still wet."

"So come talk to me while I shower," Joe commanded her. "I want you nearby." She stood up and Joe pushed the loose-fitting nightgown down her body. "I just had to see you," he explained, and he leaned down and kissed one of her nipples. "I can't resist the sight of you naked."

As Lynne watched Joe through the glass door of the shower, she admired his body but realized that the sight of him naked would have turned her on just as much if he had been skinny, or too heavy, or unattractive in some other way. She was attracted to Joe because she loved him, not only because he was handsome. And as Joe gazed at her through the glass, naked and vulnerable, she realized that he was turned on by her because he loved her, as much as by her physical attributes. And that made her very happy.

Lynne was waiting with a big, fluffy towel when Joe stepped out of the shower. "Did you enjoy the peep show?" he teased as he rubbed himself dry.

"Oh, absolutely," Lynne assured him. "Did you?"

Joe stepped back and looked her up and down. "Definitely," he said, raising his head for a kiss. Lynne bent her head as Joe's arms came up around her neck; in the midst of their passionate embrace the towel fell down at their feet, leaving nothing between them except their love for one another. "Oh, Lynne, do you realize that we'll have this for the rest of our lives?" Joe asked when he'd finally broken off the long, smoldering kiss.

Lynne nodded without speaking, finally convinced that she indeed would have Joe's love for the rest of her life. She ran her fingers through his hair and looked at him with a wordless invitation in her eyes. "Come on, woman," he said, his voice thick with desire. "I want to make you mine again."

"I want you to make me yours," Lynne said. Joe took her by the hand and led her into the bedroom. She rolled her shoulders and winced a little as she sat down on the bed.

"What's the matter?" Joe asked, sitting down beside her. "Are you sore?"

"Yes, I am," Lynne admitted. "I was tense and frustrated and I took it out on the exercise machines this afternoon."

"Were you upset about me?" Joe asked.

"That, and tired. I couldn't sleep, so I volunteered for a couple of night patrols."

"I'll make sure you sleep tonight," Joe promised. He went in the bathroom and got a bottle of lotion. "Lie down on your stomach and I'll fix up those sore muscles," he volunteered. Lynne lay down and Joe poured a little lotion onto her back. He ran his hands over the puddle and stroked her back and shoulders, lightly at first and then with more pressure.

Lynne moaned a little bit. "Oww, that hurt," she complained after Joe had increased the strength of his massage.

"You did too much," Joe scolded her gently. His hands stroked down the sides of her back, firmly yet tenderly unknotting her tightly clenched muscles. Lynne relaxed and let his hands do their work, easing the strain in her neck and shoulders. Gradually, Joe's touch became more erotic than therapeutic: he stroked the sensitive skin on her lower back and rounded the indentation of her waist before drifting lower, touching and caressing her small, firm bottom. "Do you hurt down here?"

"No, but let's pretend," Lynne said, and then his fingers began tormenting her upper thighs. "Joe, that tickles!"

"Sorry about that." He grinned. He caressed her thighs, drew an imaginary picture on the backs of her knees, and kneaded the tense muscles of her calves. "Is that better?"

"Yes, much," Lynne assured him, her breathing starting to come in short, quick puffs. Joe turned her over and poured another puddle of cream on her chest right between her breasts. "Joe, what are you doing?"

"I'm finishing what I just started." His fingers spread the fragrant lotion over her breasts, caressing first one and then the other with light, sure strokes. Lynne gasped with pleasure as he ran his palm over the tip of her nipples, rotating them in circles. His lips caressed hers gently as his hands stroked the tightness out of her shoulders. "I always finish what I start."

"I hope you start this often," Lynne said, her fingers finding and caressing the tip of his nipple in the way he loved so much. Joe ran his hand down between her breasts onto the soft skin of her stomach, where he caressed her in a gentle, circular motion.

"I can hardly wait to see you grow with my children," Joe whispered as his fingers tormented her navel, sending waves of pleasure through her midsection to the center of her desire.

Lynne looked at Joe with wide eyes. "Tonight?" she teased.

"I wish," Joe said. "No, we'd better give it a few months, at least, until we can get out of hock a little. But I do want to have children with you, Lynne. Make no mistake about that. And I hope they're all just like you."

"Oh, Joe, you don't know what it means when you say that," Lynne said. Joe bent his head and touched her lips with his, pressing their bodies together from head to foot. Lynne could feel the evidence of Joe's desire for her, the strength of his feelings for her, undisguised and powerful. Her heart overflowing with love for this man, she wanted to give him something special, to show him a little of what she felt for him. Without breaking off their kiss, she moved on top of him and lifted her lips from his. "I want to pleasure you," she said. Her hands massaged him, much as his had done to her. "I want to show you how much I do love you." Her lips followed her hands down his body, touching with her tender tongue where her hands had just caressed. Slowly, she inched down his body, smoothing his chest, his waist, his stomach, before letting herself drift toward the ultimate intimacy.

"Lynne, you don't have to," Joe murmured when he felt her hesitate just the slightest bit.

"No, I just wasn't sure you wanted me to," Lynne said, hearing the longing in his voice. Slowly she lowered her lips, caressing him unselfishly, giving him the sharpest of pleasure. Joe gave himself up, letting her take him on a roller-coaster ride of passion. Lynne caressed him until she sensed that he could take no more, and together they protected Lynne before Joe pushed her back down onto the bed and joined them together in the tender act of love.

They made love silently, reverently, using their bodies to seal the commitment they had made earlier with words. With each touch and stroke Joe showed her that he loved her, and wanted her, and desired her, as he had desired no other woman. Lynne poured out her love for Joe, tenderly conveying her feelings for him by the way she kissed and caressed him—with unbridled passion. Together they gave and took, loved and were loved, desired and had their desire fulfilled, until they were both engulfed with the searing fire of mutual ecstasy. The flame of their passion banked but by no means gone, they paused for a few minutes before Joe started moving again, slowly at first and then with increased strength, until the inferno blazed once more. They rode the crest a second time, their pleasure even more intense. Lynne cried out softly at the supreme moment, her love for Joe transporting her to a most magic place in time. Above her Joe flinched as he too reached the ultimate, and together they collapsed into a tangle of arms and legs.

They lay still, Joe's head on Lynne's shoulder. "We're going to have quite a life together, you know that?" he murmured, stroking Lynne's hair.

"Yes, I know that now," Lynne whispered, and held him close.

Joe snuggled down next to her, his head pillowed between her breasts. "Still want to go fishing for our honeymoon?"

"I'm counting on it," Lynne said sleepily, not telling Joe that she had bought him a fancy rod and reel for his wedding present from her. They talked quietly for a few minutes before Joe fell asleep in her arms.

Lynne cradled the sleeping man next to her, and her heart overflowed with love. And he did love her—he loved her a lot. Lynne smiled in the darkness, remembering the reasons he had given for having fallen in love with her. Maybe she was luckier than she had thought she was. Joe loved her for the person she was and the life he could live with her, and those were things that would not change as they grew older. Those didn't fade with time, as a pretty face or a stunning figure did. Those qualities lasted, and they would bind Joe to her for a lifetime. Finally convinced that Joe was hers, Lynne whispered a prayer of thanks into the dark night and went to sleep, confident that Joe would love her forever.

Now you can reserve March's Candlelights *before they're published!*

♥ You'll have copies set aside for *you* the instant they come off press.

♥ You'll save yourself precious shopping time by arranging for *home delivery.*

♥ You'll feel proud and efficient about organizing a system that *guarantees* delivery.

♥ You'll avoid the disappointment of not finding *every* title you want and need.

ECSTASY SUPREMES $2.75 each

☐ **113 NIGHT STRIKER,** A. Lorin 16391-9-12
☐ **114 THE WORLD IN HIS ARMS,** J. Brandon 19767-8-12
☐ **115 RISKING IT ALL,** C. Murray 17446-5-23
☐ **116 A VERY SPECIAL LOVER,** E. Elliott 19315-X-27

ECSTASY ROMANCES $2.25 each

☐ **410 SWEET-TIME LOVIN',** B. Cameron 18419-3-24
☐ **411 SING SOFTLY TO ME,** D. Phillips 17865-7-33
☐ **412 ALL A MAN COULD WANT,** L.R. Wisdom . . 10179-4-39
☐ **413 SOMETHING WILD AND FREE,** H. Conrad . . 18134-8-10
☐ **414 TO THE HIGHEST BIDDER,** N. Beach 18707-9-33
☐ **415 HANDS OFF THE LADY,** E. Randolph 13427-7-17
☐ **416 WITH EVERY KISS,** S. Paulos 19744-9-28
☐ **417 DREAM MAKER,** D.K. Vitek 12155-8-17

JAYNE CASTLE

excites and delights you with tales of adventure and romance

_____TRADING SECRETS

Sabrina had wanted only a casual vacation fling with the rugged Matt. But the extraordinary pull between them made that impossible. So did her growing relationship with his son—and her daring attempt to save the boy's life.
19053-3-15 $3.50

_____DOUBLE DEALING

Jayne Castle sweeps you into the corporate world of multimillion dollar real estate schemes and the very private world of executive lovers. Mixing business with pleasure, they made _passion_ their bottom line.
12121-3-18 $3.95

ROBERTA GELLIS

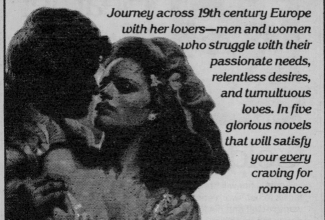

Journey across 19th century Europe with her lovers—men and women who struggle with their passionate needs, relentless desires, and tumultuous loves. In five glorious novels that will satisfy your <u>every</u> craving for romance.

You're About to Become a
Privileged Woman.

INTRODUCING
PAGES & PRIVILEGES™.

It's our way of thanking you for buying
our books at your favorite retail store.

— *GET ALL THIS FREE* —
WITH JUST ONE PROOF OF PURCHASE:

◆ **Hotel Discounts up to 60% at home and abroad**

◆ **Travel Service - Guaranteed lowest published airfares plus 5% cash back on tickets**

◆ **$25 Travel Voucher**

◆ **Sensuous Petite Parfumerie collection ($50 value)**

◆ **Insider Tips Letter with sneak previews of upcoming books**

◆ **Mystery Gift (if you enroll before 6/15/95)**

You'll get a FREE personal card, too.
It's your passport to all these benefits– and to
even more great gifts & benefits to come!

There's no club to join. No purchase commitment. No obligation.

As a Privileged Woman,
you'll be entitled to all
these Free Benefits.
And Free Gifts, too.

To thank you for buying our books, we've designed an exclusive FREE program called *PAGES & PRIVILEGES™*. You can enroll with just one Proof of Purchase, and get the kind of luxuries that, until now, you could only read about.

BIG HOTEL DISCOUNTS

A privileged woman stays in the finest hotels. And so can you—at up to 60% off! Imagine standing in a hotel check-in line and watching as the guest in front of you pays $150 for the same room that's only costing you $60. Your *Pages & Privileges* discounts are good at Sheraton, Marriott, Best Western, Hyatt and thousands of other fine hotels all over the U.S., Canada and Europe.

FREE DISCOUNT TRAVEL SERVICE

A privileged woman is always jetting to romantic places.
When <u>you</u> fly, just make one phone call for the lowest published airfare at time of booking—<u>or double the difference back</u>! PLUS—

you'll get a $25 voucher to use the first time you book a flight AND <u>5% cash back on every ticket you buy thereafter through the travel service</u>!

𝓕REE GIFTS!

$50 VALUE

A privileged woman is always getting wonderful gifts.
Luxuriate in rich fragrances that will stir your senses (and his). This gift-boxed assortment of fine perfumes includes three popular scents, each in a beautiful designer bottle. <u>Truly Lace</u>...This luxurious fragrance unveils your sensuous side. <u>L'Effleur</u>...discover the romance of the Victorian era with this soft floral. <u>Muguet des bois</u>...a single note floral of singular beauty. This $50 value is yours—FREE when you enroll in *Pages & Privileges*! And it's just the beginning of the gifts and benefits that will be coming your way!

𝓕REE INSIDER TIPS LETTER

A privileged woman is always informed. And you'll be, too, with our free letter full of fascinating information and sneak previews of upcoming books.

𝓜ORE GREAT GIFTS & BENEFITS TO COME

A privileged woman always has a lot to look forward to.
And so will you. You get all these wonderful FREE gifts and benefits now with only one purchase...and there are no additional purchases required. However, each additional retail purchase of Harlequin and Silhouette books brings you a step closer to even more great FREE benefits like half-price movie tickets...and even more FREE gifts like these beautiful fragrance gift baskets:

L'Effleur ...This basketful of romance lets you discover L'Effleur from head to toe, heart to home.

Truly Lace ...A basket spun with the sensuous luxuries of Truly Lace, including Dusting Powder in a reusable satin and lace covered box.

𝓔NROLL 𝓝OW!
Complete the Enrollment Form on the back of this card and become a Privileged Woman today!

Enroll Today in *PAGES & PRIVILEGES*™, the program that gives you Great Gifts and Benefits with just one purchase!

Enrollment Form

☐ *Yes!* I WANT TO BE A *PRIVILEGED WOMAN.*
Enclosed is one *PAGES & PRIVILEGES*™ Proof of Purchase from any Harlequin or Silhouette book currently for sale in stores (Proofs of Purchase are found on the back pages of books) and the store cash register receipt. Please enroll me in *PAGES & PRIVILEGES*™. Send my Welcome Kit and FREE Gifts -- and activate my FREE benefits -- immediately.

NAME (please print)

ADDRESS   APT. NO

CITY   STATE   ZIP/POSTAL CODE

PROOF OF PURCHASE
SAMPLE ONLY

Please allow 6-8 weeks for delivery. Quantities are limited. We reserve the right to substitute items. Enroll before October 31, 1995 and receive one full year of benefits.

**NO CLUB!
NO COMMITMENT!**
Just one purchase brings you great Free Gifts and Benefits!
(See inside for details.)

Name of store where this book was purchased_____

Date of purchase_____

Type of store:

    ☐ Bookstore ☐ Supermarket ☐ Drugstore

    ☐ Dept. or discount store (e.g. K-Mart or Walmart)

    ☐ Other (specify)_____

Which Harlequin or Silhouette series do you usually read?

_____

Complete and mail with one Proof of Purchase and store receipt to:

U.S.: *PAGES & PRIVILEGES*™, P.O. Box 1960, Danbury, CT 06813-1960

Canada: *PAGES & PRIVILEGES*™, 49-6A The Donway West, P.O. 813, North York, ON M3C 2E8   PRINTED IN U.S.A